THE FACELESS MAN

No one had seen him, yet everyone knew him. He was the administrant of ultimate justice in the province of Shant, and his name struck terror in the hearts and minds of all people.

To break canton law was to defy the Faceless Man. To leave one's canton was to defy the Faceless Man. To refuse to wear the torc that marked your birthright was to defy the Faceless Man.

Gastel Etzwane had done all three.

And to defy the Faceless Man meant death. . . .

THE ANOME

DURDANE: Book I

Jack Vance

A DELL BOOK

Published by
Dell Publishing Co., Inc.
1 Dag Hammarskjold Plaza
New York, New York 10017

Dell ® TM 681510, Dell Publishing Co., Inc.
Printed in the United States of America
First printing—March 1973

Chapter 1

At the age of nine Mur heard a man in his mother's rest cottage call out a jocular curse in the name of the Faceless Man. Later, after the man had gone his way, Mur put a question to his mother. "Is the Faceless Man real?"

"He is real, indeed," replied Eathre.

Mur considered the matter for a period, then asked, "How does he eat or smell or talk?"

Eathre, in her calm voice, replied, "I suppose one way or another he manages."

"It would be interesting to watch," said Mur.

"No doubt."

"Have you ever seen him?"

Eathre shook her head. "The Faceless Man never troubles the Chilites, so you need not concern yourself for the Faceless Man." She added as a musing afterthought: "For better or worse, such is the case."

Mur, a child thin and somber, knit the black brows that had come as a legacy from his unknown blood-father. "Why should such a case be better? Or worse?"

"What a vexatious child you are!" declared Eathre without heat. Her lips twitched: perhaps a twinge of *chsein*.* But she said, "If a person breaks Chilite law, the Ecclesiarchs punish him.

---

* *Chsein:* (1) Conditioned recoil from a forbidden thought. (2) Blindness or obliviousness to the actuality of unfamiliar, forbidden, or unorthodox circumstances.

If he runs away, the Faceless Man takes his head." Eathre's hand went to her torc, a mannerism common to all the folk of Shant. "If you obey Chilite law, you need never fear the loss of your head. This is the 'better.' In such a case, however, you are a Chilite, and this is the 'worse.' "

Mur said no more. The remarks were unsettling. Were his soul-father to hear, Eathre would incur at least a reprimand. She might be transferred to the tannery, and Mur's world would be shattered. The time left him "on mother's milk" (to use the Chilite idiom) was short enough in any event: three or four years. . . . A wayfarer entered the cottage. Earthre put a garland of flowers around her brow and poured a goblet of wine.

Mur went to sit in the shade of the great rhododendrons across the Way. To some such encounter he owed his existence, so he was aware; an Original Guilt that he must expiate when he became a Chilite Pure Boy. The whole process taxed his mind. Eathre had borne four children. Delamber, a girl of sixteen, already maintained a cottage at the west end of the Way. The second child, Blink, three years older than Mur, had already put on the white robe of a Pure Boy and had assumed the name Chalres Gargamet, combining the virtues of Chalres, the Chilite ascetic who had lived and died in the branches of the Holy Oak, four miles up Mirk Valley, and Bastin Gargamet, the master tanner who (while fuming ahulph* hides) had discovered the sacramental

---

* Ahulph: a half-intelligent biped autochthonous to Durdane, ranging wild in the backlands and wildernesses, on occasion tamed, bred and crossbred for a variety of uses, from unskilled labor and portage to house pets. When

qualities of galga.* The fourth child, born two years after Mur, had been adjudged defective and drowned in the tannery sump, with prejudice toward Eathre, sexual eccentricity being held the cause of fetal defects.

Mur sat under the rhododendrons scratching patterns in the white dust and appraising those who passed: a mercantilist driving a pacer-trap rented at the balloon-way station in Canton Seamus, then three young vagabonds; agricultural workers by the green-brown verticals of their torc-badges.

Mur stirred himself. His plot of fiber-trees wanted tending; if the bobbins were allowed to run slack, the thread became lumpy and coarse. . . . A steam-powered dray came past, loaded with fine long black-wood timbers. Mur, forgetting fiber-trees, gave chase and hung dangling from the end timber all the way to Mirk Bridge where he dropped onto the road and watched the dray rumble along the far wild road to the east. For a period he dropped pebbles into the Mirk; just above the bridge turned a waterwheel to grind galls, alum, dye-stone, all manner of herbs, roots, and chemicals for the tannery.

Mur idled back along Rhododendron Way, and found the traveler departed. Eathre set out bread and soup for his lunch. As Mur ate, he asked the question that all morning had been tugging at a corner of his mind. "Chalres resembles his soul-

---

sick, the ahulph exudes a detestable odor that excites even itself to complaint.
* Galga: Dried leaves of the easil bush, pulverized, bound with easil gum and ahulph blood: an important adjunct to the spasmic Chilite worship of Galexis.

father, but I do not; isn't this strange?"

Eathre paused for knowledge to well up into her mind: a wonderful elemental process, like the flowering of trees or juice oozing from bruised fruit. "Neither you nor Chalres have blood-connection with Grand Male Osso or any other Chilite. They have no knowledge of real women. Chalres's father I do not know. Your blood-father was a wanderer, a music-maker, one of those who travel alone. I was sorry when he went his way."

"He never came back?"

"Never."

"Where did he go?"

Eathre shook her head. "Such as Dystar wander all the cantons of Shant."

"And you could not go with him?"

"Not while Osso holds my indenture."

Mur ate his soup in thoughtful silence.

Into the cottage came Delamber, a cloak over her striped gown of green and blue. Like Mur, she was slender and serious; like her mother, she was tall and as softly even as a flowing river. She sank into a chair. "Already I am tired; I have had three musicians from the camp. The last was most difficult and full of talk as well. He decided to tell me of certain barbarians, the Roguskhoi: great drunkards and great lechers. Have you heard of them?"

"Yes," said Eathre. "The man who just now departed regards them with great respect. He described their lust as beyond the usual, from which no woman is safe, nor do they pay."

"Why doesn't the Faceless Man drive them away?" demanded Mur.

"Wild folk wear no torcs; the Faceless Man

can't deal with them. In any event they have been beaten back and are no longer considered a threat."

Eathre served tea; Mur took two nut-cakes and went out into the garden behind the cottage where he heard the voice of Chalres, his soul-brother.

Mur looked around without enthusiasm. Down the hillside sauntered Chalres, halting at the edge of the garden where he dared not venture for fear of defilement. Chalres, who bore no re-semblance to Mur, was thin and tall, with small sharp features in constant agitation. His eyes blinked, bulged, screwed up, rolled right and left; his nose twitched; he grinned, grimaced, sneered, showed his teeth, licked his lips, guf-fawed when a chuckle might have sufficed; he scratched his nose, rubbed his ears, made wide, ungainly gestures. Mur had long wondered why he and Chalres differed in so many attributes. Did they not share the same mother, the same soul-father? To some extent Chalres resembled their mutual soul-father Great Male Osso, who was himself tall, sallow, and thin as a bell-ringer.

"Come along," said Chalres, "you are to pick berries."

"I to pick berries? Who said I must?"

"I say so, and to ensure purity from woman-taint, I have brought sacramental gloves for you. Take care to breathe off to the side and all will be well. What is that you are eating?"

"Nut-cakes."

"Hmmf . . . I have had nothing this morning but biscuit and water. . . . No. I dare not. Osso would learn. He has a nose like an ahulph. Here, take this." He tossed Mur a basket containing white gloves: Chalres's own, Mur suspected, which even as a Pure Boy he was required to wear while handling food. Chalres, it seemed, valued his ease more than he feared defiling the food, which was for the Chilites' table, in any event.

Mur, while not overly fond of Chalres, felt a certain sympathy for his privations; in so short a time they would be inflicted on Mur himself. He took the basket without protest: if the fraud were discovered it was Chalres who would pay. He asked grudgingly, "Do you want a nut-cake? Or not?"

Chalres searched the hillside, the white bulk of Bashon Temple, the row of dark bays under the walls where the Pure Boys made their dens. "Come over to the apar tree."

Behind the apar tree Chalres ceremoniously donned the white gloves. Taking the nut-cake, he devoured it in a gulp. Then, licking the crumbs from his cheeks, he performed a set of uneasy grimaces, coughing, twitching his nose, peering up the hillside. At last, reassured, he made a grand gesture to wipe the whole affair from memory.

The two set off toward the berry patch at the western end of Rhododendron Way, Chalres pointedly maintaining a distance between himself and his unpurified soul-brother.

"Tonight the Ecclesiarchs meet in Doctrinal Conclave," Chalres told Mur with the air of one imparting important news. "They make a dessert of berries, and a great basket is required. Would you believe it? I have been sent forth alone to pluck this massive quantity. For all the delicacy of their ideals and the rigor of their determination, they consume every bite put before them."

"Hah," said Mur in saturnine deprecation. "How long until your own assumption?"

"A year. Already I grow body hair."

"Do you realize that once they clap a torc around your neck, you may never again roam or wander?"

Chalres sniffed. "That is like saying: Once a tree is grown, it may not become a seed again."

"Then you don't care to wander?"

Chalres gave a grumbling elliptical answer. "Wanderers wear torcs as well. Show me a wanderer without a torc and I will show you an outlander."

Mur had no ready response. Presently he asked: "The Roguskhoi: are they outlanders?"

"The what? I've never heard of them."

Mur, with little more knoweldge than Chalres, judiciously said no more. Passing the tree-silk plantation, where Mur tended a plot of two hundred bobbins, they descended to the berry patch. Chalres halted and glanced back up toward the temple. "Look now; you go yonder, around and below to the low patch; I'll harvest above, where those of the temple can observe and approve, should they feel the inclination. Mind you, wear the gloves! This is the minimum precaution I can countenance."

"What of Osso's minimum?"

"As to that we can only speculate. I need at least two basketfuls, so work at speed. Don't forget the gloves! The Chilites detect woman-taint farther than an ordinary man smells smoke."

Mur descended to the lower verge of the berry patch where he made a further detour to inspect

the camp of the musicians. This was an unusually large troupe, comprising seven wagons, each
painted in patterns of meaningful colors: light
blue for gaiety, pink for innocence, dark yellow
for *sunuschein,** gray-brown to affirm technical
competence.

The troupe was busy with camp routine: tending the draft animals, cutting vegetables into
cauldrons, flapping out shawls and blankets. As a
group they were considerably more effusive and
volatile than the Chilites; their gestures were
abrupt and often flamboyant; when they laughed,
they threw back their heads; even the chronical-
ly surly evinced their ill nature in unmistakable
poses. An old man sat on the steps of a wagon
fitting new pegs to a small crooknecked khitan.
Nearby a boy about Mur's own age practiced the
gastaing, striking runs and arpeggios while the
old man called gruff advice.

Mur sighed and, turning away, climbed the
slope into the berry patch. Ahead of him a blotch
of pale brown shifted and flickered; there was a
sound of rustling leaves. Mur stopped short, then
slowly advanced. Peering through the foliage,
he discovered a girl a year or two older than himself picking berries with great deftness, filling the
basket slung over her arm.

Indignant at the girl's trespass, Mur strode forward, tripped on a dead branch, and crashed
down into a hag-bush. The girl turned half a
startled glance over her shoulder, dropped her
basket, and ran pell-mell through the berry patch,

* *Sunuschein:* reckless, feckless gaiety, tinged with fatal-
ism and tragic despair.

skirt hiked up to her thighs. Mur hoisted himself
foolishly to his feet. He looked after the girl. He
had not meant to frighten her, but since the deed
was done, so be it! Scratched legs or not, she had
no business among the Chilite berries. He picked
up the basket she had dropped and with careful
malice poured the berries into his own basket.
Here were berries for the Conclave!

Thrusting the gloves into his pocket, he picked
for a period, working up the slope. Presently
Chalres hailed him. "Boy! Where are the berries?
Have you toiled or loitered?"

"See for yourself," said Mur.

Chalres peered into the basket, pointedly ignoring the fact that Mur wore no gloves. "Hmm.
You've done quite well. Surprising. Well, then,
pour them in here. I'll say that's all there were to
be had. . . . Excellent. Ah yes, the gloves. You
are exceedingly neat." Chalres crushed a berry
between the fingers of the glove. "That looks
somewhat better. Now, then, no tales." He shoved
his thin face fiercely into Mur's. "Remember, when
you're a Pure Boy, I'll be a Chilite—and much
sterner than I am now, for I can see that this is
how the tide runs!" He returned up the hill to the
temple.

With nothing better to do, Mur picked a few
more berries for his mother, eating as many as he
dropped into the basket. Presently, as he had half-
expected, the pale brown smock of the wanderer
girl appeared somewhat down the slope. He approached slowly, making sure that she heard
him, and this time she showed no disposition to
flee. Instead, she came running forward, face
glowing with rage. "You little weirdling, you

frightened me; you took my berries! Where are they now? Give them here before I pull those ridiculous ears of yours!"

Mur, somewhat taken aback, strove to maintain an imperturbable Chilite dignity. "You need not call names."

"I need to do so very much! How else should I address a thief?"

"You are the thief; these are Chilite berry grounds!"

The girl threw up her hands and gave a petulant exclamation. "Who the thief and who not the thief? It's all one, so long as I have my berries." She snatched away Mur's basket, looked askance at the handful she found there. "Was that all I had picked?"

"There were more," declared Mur with stately candor. "I gave them to my soul-brother. Don't be annoyed; they go to the Chilite Conclave. Isn't it a great joke? A woman has defiled the food!"

The girl once again became angry. "I defiled no food! What do you take me for?"

"Perhaps you don't understand that—"

"Indeed not, and I never will! Not the Chilites! I know your dirty ways! You drug yourselves with smoke and dream lewd dreams; there never was so odd a sect!"

"The Chilites are not a sect," stated Mur, reciting the doctrine he had heard from Chalres. "I can tell you little because as of yet I am not even a 'Pure Boy' and won't have full control of my soul for another three or four years. The Chilites are the single emancipated and high-cultured folk of Durdane. All other folk live by emotion; the Chilites maintain an abstract and intellectual existence."

The girl gave an offensive laugh. "You infant! What do you know of other folk? You haven't set foot a hundred yards down the road in either direction."

Mur could not refute the jibe. "Well, I have learned from the men who come to my mother's cottage. And never forget, my blood-father was a musician!"

"Indeed? What was his name?"

"Dystar."

"Dystar . . . Come over to the wagons. I'll learn the truth about your father, what manner of musician he was."

Mur's heart beat faster; he drew back. "I'm not sure I want to know."

"Why not? What are you afraid of?"

"I'm afraid of nothing. I am a Chilite, and consequently—"

"Yes, yes; come along, then."

On leaden legs Mur followed, trying to strike upon some convincing reason why he should not go into the musician's camp. The girl looked back, showing a bold and saucy grin, and finally Mur became annoyed. She took him for a liar and a freak, did she? Nothing could dissuade him now. . . . They entered the musicians' camp. "Azouk, Azouk!" cried a woman. "Are there berries? Bring them here."

"No berries," stated Azouk in disgust. "This little thief took them from me. I brought him here for a hiding."

"Come now," said the woman. "Do you have berries or no?"

The girl gave over the near-empty basket with a flourish. "It is as I said. This freaklet took them and claims beside his father was a musician—a certain Dystar."

"Well, and why not? Are musicians unlike other men? Beget and forget, that's how it goes." And she added, "His mother must be a methodical woman."

Mur essayed a timid question. "Did you know my father Dystar?"

The woman jerked her finger. "Ply the old man with the broken khitan. He knows every drunken musician of Shant. Come, you Azouk! Must you idle away your life, you hussy? Fetch twigs and foster the fire!" The woman went off to stir a cauldron; with a saucy toss of the head, the girl disappeared behind a wagon. Mur stood alone. No one needed him. All the folk of the troupe worked with intense concentration, as if their immediate task were the most important act they would ever undertake. In all the camp the old man seemed the most relaxed, and even he worked with zestful flourishes of his elbows and intermittent pauses to scowl down at his handiwork. Step by step Mur approached. The old man flicked him a cool glance and began to fit a string to the crooknecked khitan.

Mur watched in respectful silence. As the old man worked, he hissed a tune through his teeth. He dropped his awl; Mur picked it up and handed it to him, and received another side glance. Mur moved a step closer.

"Well, then," demanded the old man in a challenging voice, "do you consider the job well done?"

After a moment's hesitation Mur said, "I would think so. However, at Bashon we see few musical instruments. The Chilites prefer what they call a 'clear, cold silence.' My soul-father, Osso Higajou, is disturbed by the tinkle of a bell-bug."

The old man paused in his work. "That seems a peculiar circumstance. What of yourself? Are you a Chilite?"

"No, not yet. I live with my mother Eathre, half along the Way. I'm not sure I want to be a Chilite."

"And why not? They live easy enough, in 'clear, cool silence,' with all their women to toil for them."

Mur nodded sagely. "Yes, I suppose that's true . . . But first I'd have to be a Pure Boy, and I don't really want to leave my mother. Also my blood-father was a musician. His name was Dystar."

"Dystar." The old man tautened the new string and gave it a touch. "Yes; I know of Dystar. A druithine."

Mur moved closer. "What is a druithine?"

"He is one who does not go with a troupe. He wanders by himself; he carries a khitan, such as this, or perhaps a gastaing; thus he is able to import his wisdom and the circumstances of his life."

"He sings?"

"Ah no, no indeed! No singing. That is for minstrels and balladeers. We do not reckon singing to be music; it is another matter entirely. Ha ha, what would Dystar have said to that!"

"What kind of a man is Dystar?"

The old man thrust his face forward; Mur jumped a step back. The old man demanded: "Why do you ask this, you who are to become a Pure Boy?"

"I have often wondered about my father."

"Very well, I will tell you. He was a strong,

harsh-faced man. He played with passion, and
there was never any doubt as to his feelings. And
do you know how he died?"

"I did not know he was dead."

"This is how the story goes. One night he became furiously drunk. He played* the gastaing,
and all who heard were deeply moved. After-
wards, so it is told, he ran out into the street, rav-
ing that his torc choked him, and some saw him
wrenching at it. Whether he broke it and took his
own head, or whether the Faceless Man came by
and disapproved, it is not known; but in the
morning his body was found, and the wonderful
head, so full of tunes, was gone." The old man
gave a fretful tug at his own torc. Mur noted his
colors: horizontals of purple and rose, indicating
lack of cantonal affiliation; verticals of gray and
brown, musicians' colors; a personal code of blue,
dark green, dark yellow, scarlet, blue and purple.
Mur felt his own neck, as yet naked. How would
it feel to be clamped with a torc? Some said
that for months, or even years, a person felt stifled, in constant dread; Mur had heard of cases
where the person clamped became frantic and
broke the torc apart, taking his own head. Mur
licked his lips. The torcs were necessary, but
sometimes he wished he might remain a child and
live with his mother in a pleasant cottage far
from Bashon and never be troubled by torc or
Chilite or Faceless Man or anyone.

The old man stroked the khitan, producing a
wistful set of chords. Mur watched the agile fin-

---

* *Played:* a feeble rendering of the Shant verb *zuweshekar:*
to use a musical instrument with such passion that the
music takes on a life of its own.

gers with fascination. The tempo increased, the melody jumped this way and that. . . . The old man stopped playing. "That was a jig of Barbado, which is a seaport to the south of Canton Enterland. How did you like it?"

"Very much."

The old man grunted. "Take this khitan for your own. Tomorrow, steal me a pelt of good leather, or pick me a bucket of berries, or send me only your good wishes—I do not care."

"I'll do all three!" cried Mur. "And more, if you ask! But how can I learn the sleight?"

"No great matter if you strive. To alter key, bend the neck; you need learn but a single set of chords; the complete schedule is carved on the back. As how to use the chords, that is a different matter and derives from skill and long experience of music and life." He raised his finger portentously high. "When you become a great druithine, remember that your first khitan came from Feld Maijesto."

Mur held the instrument awkwardly. "I know no tunes; at Bashon there is no music."

"Contrive your own tunes!" snapped the old man. "Further, don't let soul-father Osso hear you; don't ask him to sing to your music or you'll learn the meaning of trouble!"

Mur departed the musicians' camp, his head effervescent with joy and wonder and disbelief for the marvelous thing that had happened to him.

Stepping into the Way, he came to his senses and stopped short. To carry this khitan home in full view was to start gossip along a route leading to his soul-father. Osso would instantly order the instrument destroyed as an article at odds with the spare Chilite doctrines.

By a devious route behind the rhododendrons, Mur returned to the cottage of his mother. She showed no surprise at the sight of the khitan, nor did Mur expect any of her. He told her all that had happened to him and reported the death of Dystar. She looked off into the dusk, for the suns had set, and the sky was purple. "Just such a way Dystar was fated to die; and after all it was not so bad." She touched her own torc and, turning away, prepared Mur's supper, taking special pains to please him.

Even so, Mur was distraught. "Must we always wear torcs? Couldn't folk agree to behave well so that there was no need?"

Eathre shook her head sadly. "I have heard that only lawbreakers resent the torc; as to this, I can't say. On the day the torc clamped my neck, I felt cramped and broken and awry. Perhaps there are better ways; I don't know. Soon you will be gone from me; I would not hinder you, whatever the way of your life, but to bless Saccard I must damn Saccume.* I hardly know what to tell you."

At Mur's expression of bewilderment Eathre said, "Very well, listen then. I counsel you to resourcefulness: defeat adversities rather than accept them! Strive for excellence! You must try to do better than the best, even if it means a lifetime of dissatisfaction for your own inadequacy!"

Mur tested the ideas. "I must learn rites and rotes better than anyone else? Better than

---

* Saccard and Saccume: protagonists of a thousand Shant fables, always at odds, or working against each other, or the victims of antithetical circumstances.

Chalres? Better than Neech when he becomes a Pure Boy? So that I will become an Ecclesiarch?"

Eathre was a long time answering. "If you are eager to become an Ecclesiarch, this is what you must do."

Mur, who knew every subtle intonation of his mother's voice, nodded slowly.

"But now you must go to bed," said Eathre. "Mind when you play the khitan! Muffle the strings, take the fibers from the rattle-box. Otherwise Osso will have me at the tannery before my time."

In the darkness Mur stroked the strings, shivering at the soft sounds. He would never be a Pure Boy; he and his mother would run away, they would become musicians! But, ah no, Eathre could not run away! She was indentured. How could he go without her? Never! So then—what? He clutched the khitan to his breast.

The morning brought news of a terrible circumstance. Face down in the tannery sludge, the body of Chalres Gargamet was discovered. How he had died was uncertain, though his arms and legs were peculiarly twisted, like those of an antic dancer.

Somewhat later, whispers seeped from cottage to cottage. On the previous day Chalres had picked berries for the Conclave. Among the berries, after he had eaten, Great Male Osso had found a long black woman-hair. And those who whispered to each other felt quivering chills of that curious emotion that is half horror and half appreciation of some grotesque absurdity. As for Mur, he became deathly pale and slumped into the darkest corner of the cottage where he lay limp, with only the twitch of his narrow shoulder blades to indicate that he was alive.

At dusk Eathre covered Mur with a quilt and allowed him to lie quiet, though all night both lay awake. In the morning she brought him gruel. He turned up his thin face, lips trembling, hair matted. Eathre blinked back her tears and hugged him. Mur began to keen: a low wailing sound deep in his throat that slowly rose in pitch. Eathre shook him gently. "Mur, Mur, Mur!"

Later in the day Mur touched the khitan: an uninterested stroke of the fingers. He could not slip into the tannery warehouse for a pelt; he could not pick a basket of berries; he tried to transmit a complement of kind thoughts, but they seemed pallid and weak.

At sunset Eathre brought him stewed fruit and tea; Mur at first shook his head, then listlessly ate. Eathre stood looking down at him—for so long a period that Mur raised his eyes. She said, "Before you assume to Soul, if you go from Bashon, they can't denounce you to the Faceless Man. If you like, I will find a kind man to take you for apprentice."

"They would set ahulphs after us."

"The matter could be arranged."

Mur shook his head. "I don't care to leave you."

"When you become a Chilite, you leave me, and worse."

"Even then I won't leave you! They can kill me, but still I won't."

Eathre stroked his head. "Chilite or dead, we would still be apart. Is this not true?"

"I will see you secretly. I can arrange that you need not work so hard."

"The work is not all that dreadful," said Eathre softly. "Everywhere women must work."

"The Faceless Man must be a monster!" cried Mur in a husky voice.

"No!" exclaimed Eathre with as much agitation as her temperament allowed. She reflected for a moment, composing her limpid thoughts. "How can I explain? You are so young! Human beings change with the minute! The man who praises Saccard may rage like a sick ahulph at Saccume. Do you understand? Men are perverse and cannot be predicted. To live without dissension they bind themselves by rules. Each of the sixty-two cantons uses a different set of rules. Which are the best, which the worst? No one knows, and perhaps it doesn't matter if only men abide by any one of these sets. If they don't—the others call out his colors to the Faceless Man. Or perhaps a monitor files a derogation. Or sometimes the Faceless Man comes wandering, or he sends his Benevolences, as quiet as the Faceless Man himself. Do you now understand? The Faceless Man merely enforces the laws of the folk of Shant: those they have made for themselves."

"I suppose this is so," said Mur. "Still, if I were the Faceless Man, I would abolish fear and hardship, and you would never work at the tannery."

Eathre stroked his head. "Yes, dear Mur, I know. You would force men to be kind and good and cause a great disaster. Go to sleep now; the world will be much the same tomorrow."

Chapter 2

On a cool morning in the fall of the year a Pure Boy came down to the boundary and called for Mur. "Your soul-father will see you at noon, at the portal to the under-room. Cleanse yourself well."

With leaden motions, Mur bathed, dressed in a clean smock. Eathre watched from the far side of the room, not wishing to contribute woman-taint to Mur's nervousness.

At last she could not restrain herself and came to brush down his stubborn black hair. "Remember, he only wants to gauge your growth and speak to you of Chilite doctrine. There is nothing whatever to fear."

"That may be so," said Mur. "Still, I am afraid."

"Nonsense," said Eathre decidedly. "You are not afraid; you are the brave Mur. Listen carefully; obey exactly; answer cautious words to his questions; do nothing eccentric."

At the cottage door she brought an ember from the fire and blew smoke through Mur's clothes and hair so at least not to prejudice Osso with woman-taint.

Ten minutes before noon Mur set out for the temple, taut with foreboding. The road seemed a lonely place; white dust rose in his footsteps to eddy in the lavender sunlight. Above bulked the temple: a set of squat convex cylinders, gradually filling the sky. With the flow of cool air down the hill came the reek of stale galga.

Mur circled the base of the temple to a stall-like half-room open to the sky: a place known as the under-room, now empty. Mur arranged himself primly by the wall and waited.

Time passed. The suns climbed the sky, the blaze of white Sasetta passing across the plum-red haunch of Ezeletta, blue Zael on the round-about: three dwarf stars dancing through space like fireflies.

Mur mused across the countryside. He could see far, far, far, in all directions: west to Canton Seamus; north to Shimrod Forest and beyond to Canton Ferriy where the folk made ironweb on their red hillsides.

A sound startled him. He jerked around to find Osso frowning down from a high pulpit. Mur had made a poor beginning; rather than waiting in a crouch of timorous reverence, here he stood gazing over the panorama.

For a minute or longer Osso looked down at Mur, who stared back in fascination. Osso spoke in a voice of sepulchral gravity: "Have the girls made ignoble play with you?"

The language was ambiguous; Mur understood the semantic content. He swallowed harder, recalling incidents that might be construed as ignoble play. He said, "No, never."

"Have you suggested or initiated vile concatenations with the female girls?"

"No," quavered Mur. "Never."

Osso gave a curt nod. "From your present age forward you must take care. You will shortly become a Pure Boy, thereafter a Chilite. Do not complicate the already rigorous rituals."

Mur gave an acquiescent mumble.

"You can expedite your passage into the temple," spoke Osso. "Devour no greasy food, drink no syrups nor baklavy. The bond between child and mother is strong; now is the time to start the solvent process. Gently disengage yourself! When your mother offers sweetmeats or attempts fond caresses, you must say, 'Madam, I am on the verge of purification; please do not add to the rigors I must endure.' Is this clear?"

"Yes, soul-father."

"You must start to forge the strongest of all bonds, the holy link to the temple. Galexis, the nervous essence, corresponds to female women as the candy of unmel to tannery sludge; you will learn more of this. Meanwhile, strengthen yourself!"

"How am I to do this?" Mur ventured.

Osso turned down a frightening glance; Mur shrank back. Osso spoke. "You know the nature of animal appetites. Philosophically—this is a doctrine you are not yet prepared to receive—they are First Order gratifications. Your belly is empty; you fill it with bread: the most crude reply to a crude sensation. The Second Order response is to consume a varied meal; at the Third Order the viands are prepared in a subtle and expert fashion to an exacting set of standards. At the Fourth Order the demands of the stomach itself are ignored; the taste nerves are stimulated by essences and extracts. At the Fifth Order the sensations occur cerebrally, completely bypassing the glottal and olfactory apparatus. At the Sixth Order the Chilite is in a state of unconscious exaltation, and sublime Galexis Achiliadnid deals directly with the soul. Is all clear? I use the simplest and most obvious example as a basis for discussion."

"I understand this all very well," said Mur. "But I am puzzled. When Chilites put food into their mouths, what is the correct doctrine on this?"

"We sustain the energy of our bodies," intoned Osso. "The style of victual, coarse or fine, is a matter of indifference. Be firm with yourself. Direct your mind from the assault of the brute appetite; find some abstract occupation upon which to focus your attention. I tied heraldic knots with imaginary cords; another Ecclesiarch, a Six-Spasm, memorized prime numbers. There are many such occupations to which you can put your mind."

"I know just the thing," said Mur with something like enthusiasm. "I will consider musical sounds."

"Use whatever device you find helpful," said Osso. "So, then, be guided. I can counsel, but progress must be made by yourself. Have you given thought to your male name?"

"Not yet, soul-father."

"It is not too early to do so. A proper name can be inspirational and exalting. In due course I will offer a list of suggestions; but for today, that is all."

Mur returned down the hill. Eathre was busy in the cottage; he wandered west along Rhododendron Way to the camp that the musicians had long vacated. Feeling hungry, he went up into the berry thicket, picked and ate berries with no thought for Osso's adjurations to abstraction.

Then he looked up the hill to the temple complex and stared a full five minutes. Somewhere in his mind cogitation occurred; he was aware of no train of ideas, but presently he made a sound in his throat, something between a laugh and a contemptuous snort.

When he returned to the cottage, Eathre was drinking tea. Mur thought that she seemed tired and wan. She asked, "How went the meeting with soul-father Osso?"

Mur grimaced. "He told me to practice purity. I am not to play with girls."

Eathre silently sipped her tea.

"He told me to curb my appetites. I am also to take a name."

Eathre acquiesced. "You are old enough to name yourself a name. What will it be?"

Mur gave a glum shrug. "Soul-father will send me down a list."

"He did the same for Glynet's son Neech."

"Did Neech take a name?"

"He called himself Geacles Vonoble."

"Hmf. And who were they?"

Eathre said tonelessly: "Geacles was the architect of the temple; Vonoble composed the Achili-adnid Dithyrambs."

"Hmf. So I must call fat Neech Geacles."

"That is now his name."

Four days later a Pure Boy pushed a long stick across the boundary with a paper in its cleft end. "A missive from Great Male Osso."

Mur took the paper into the cottage and with occasional help from Eathre puzzled out the sense of the characters. His face grew longer and longer as he read: "Bougozonie, the Seven-Spasm Ecclesiarch. Narth Homank, who ate but one nut and one berry each day. Higajou, who reorganized Pure Boy training. Faman Cocile, who allowed himself to be gelded by Shimrod Forest bandits rather than alter his creed of nonviolence and peace. Borgad Polveitch who denounced the Ambisexual Heresy." At last Mur put aside the paper.

"What is your selection?" asked Eathre.

"I can't make up my mind."

Three months later Mur was summoned to a second conference with his soul-father at the under-room. Osso again advised Mur on particularities of conduct. "It is not too early to begin carrying yourself in the style of a Pure Boy. Each day put aside one adjunct of your old child's life. Study the child's Principary, with which you will be supplied. You have selected a name for yourself?"

"Yes," said Mur.

"And what is your male name to be?"

"I now call myself Gastel Etzwane."

" 'Gastel Etzwane!' Where in the name of everything extraordinary did you derive this nomenclature?"

Mur spoke placatingly. "Well—naturally I considered your suggestions, but I thought I would like to be someone different. A man who passed along Rhododendron Way gave me a book called *Heroes of Old Shant,* and here I found my names."

"And who is 'Gastel?' And who is 'Etzwane?' "

Mur, or Gastel Etzwane, as was now his name, looked uncertainly up at his soul-father, in whom he had expected familiarity with these magic personalities. "Gastel built a great glider of withe and web and launched himself from Mount Haghead, intending to fly the breadth of Shant, but when he came to Cape Merse, rather than alighting, he sailed on over the Purple Ocean toward Caraz* and was never seen again. . . . Etzwane was the greatest musician ever to wander Shant."

Osso was silent for half a minute, seeking words. At last he spoke, in ponderous opprobium: "A crazy aeronaut and a tune-twanger: these are then your exemplars. I have failed to inculcate in you the proper ideals; I have been remiss, and it is clear that I must, in your case, exert myself more energetically. Your name is not to be Gaswane Etzel, or whatever. It shall be Faman Bougozonie, whose attributes are immeasurably more relevant and inspiring. That is all for today."

Mur—he refused to think of himself as Faman Bougozonie—returned downslope, past the tannery, where he loitered to watch the old women at their tasks, then slowly proceeded home.

Eathre asked, "Well, then, and how did it go today?"

Mur said, "I told him my name was Gastel Etzwane; he said, no, it was Faman Bougozonie."

Eathre laughed, and Mur looked at her in melancholy accusation.

Eathre became sober. She said, "A name means nothing; let him call you what he wants. You'll quickly get used to it. And to the life of a Chilite."

Mur turned away. He brought out the khitan and touched the strings. After a few moments he attempted a melody, with accents from the rattle-

---

* Caraz: (1) A color, mottled, of black, maroon, plum, with a dusting or sheen of silver-gray; symbolic of chaos and pain, macabre events in general. (2) The largest of Durdane's three continents.

box. Eathre listened approvingly, but presently Mur halted and inspected the instrument with disfavor. "I know so little, so few tunes. I can't strike the side-strings or use the brilliancy buttons or the slurs."

"Skill doesn't come easily," said Eathre. "Patience, patience. . . ."

Chapter 3

At the age of twelve, Mur, Faman Bougozonie, Gastel Etzwane—the names mingled in his mind—underwent Purification. In company with three other boys, Geacles, Morlark, and Illan, he was shorn skin-bald, then washed in the bitterly cold water of the sacred stream that welled up below the temple. After the first submersion the boys lathered themselves with aromatic tincture and once again submitted themselves to the bone-wrenching chill. Clammy, naked, shivering, the boys marched into a room heavy with the smoke of burning agapanthus. From holes in the stone floor steam arose; in a mixture of steam and smoke the boys gasped, sweated, coughed, and presently began to totter. One by one they stumbled to the floor; when the doors opened, they barely were able to raise their heads.

The voice of the Chilite supervising the Purification rang through the air: "To your feet, back to the clean water! Are you of such soft fiber? Let me see who wants to make a Chilite of himself!"

Mur struggled erect. One other boy, Geacles Vonoble, did likewise and, swaying, clutched at Mur. Both fell. Mur brought himself once more erect and helped Geacles to his feet. Geacles pushed Mur aside and loped splayfooted to the pool. Mur stood gazing with numb horror at the other two boys. Morlark lay with eyes bulging, a trickle of blood leaking from his mouth. Illan seemed unable to control his movements. Mur leaned forward, but the bland voice of the monstrator halted him. "To the pool as fast as possible! You are being watched and gauged."

Mur tottered to the pool and gave himself to the chill. His skin felt dead; his arms and legs were heavy and stiff as iron posts. He dragged himself up on the stone an inch at a time and somehow stumbled along a white-tiled passage into a chamber lined with benches. Here sat Geacles, swathed in a white robe, well satisfied with himself.

The monstrator tossed a similar robe to Mur. "Your skins are flushed of stain; for the first time since the necessary depravity of birth you are clean. Attention then to Argument One of the Chilite Procourse! Man enters the world through the genital portal: an original taint which by cleansings and attitudes the Chilite casts aside, like a serpent molting a skin, but which ordinary men carry like a stinking incubus all the way to their graves. Drink!" He handed each boy a beaker of thick liquid; they drank. "Your first purge. . . ."

Mur spent three days in a cell, with cold sacred water for sustenance. At the end of this time he was required to enter the sacred well, lather himself with tincture, and rinse. More dead than alive, he crept out into the sunlight a Pure Boy.

The monstrator gave him succinct instructions. "I need not detail the strictures; you are familiar with them. If you taint yourself, you must undergo a new Purification. I advise against it. Osso Higajou is your soul-father and not the least rigorous of the Chilites. He deplores the most trivial contact with the Female Principle. I have known him to berate a Pure Boy for enjoying the fragrance of a flower. 'The flower is a female procreative organ of the plant'—so Great Male Osso exclaimed—'and there you stand with your nose pushed into it.' Trust Osso Higajou to guide you in the Rotes. Think purity, live purity, and make sure that Great Male Osso recognizes your purity! So now—to your bay in the lower compound. You will find there wafers and porridge. Eat in moderation; tonight, meditate."

Mur went to the bay—an alcove in an openended chamber under the temple walls—and gulped down the food. The suns danced below the horizon; the sky became purple, then starshot black. Mur lay down on his back, wondering what to make of his new existence. He felt intensely alert; by some unnamable faculty he seemed to know the precise condition of every person of Bashon.

Geacles Vonoble sat across the chamber in his own bay and pretended not to notice Mur. The two were alone. Morlark and Illan had not yet completed their purification; the more advanced Pure Boys were at the evening Beatitudes. Mur considered going across to Geacles's bay for conversation but was deterred by Geacles's posture, one of pious reverie. Geacles was at once brittle and devious, affable and intent. He was not a handsome lad, with puffy cheeks and a plump torso on long thin legs. His yellow-brown eyes were round as a bird's and avid for sight, as if Geacles could never have all the seeing he wanted. Mur decided definitely against seeking Geacles's company.

He left his bay and went out to sit at the base of the temple wall. Halfway up the sky glistened a

great irregular clot of light, sparked with fifty
first-magnitude stars, the night sky's most notable
object. It cast a pallid light and created shadows
blacker than black: the Skiaffarilla, which figured
in the history of Durdane. Some said that Earth,
the legendary home of men, lay beyond the Skiaffarilla. From within the chamber came Geacles's
voice reciting aloud an Achiliadnid ode. Mur listened a moment. In spite of his fatigue, in spite
of the monstrator's warnings, in spite of Great
Male Osso, Mur would have slipped off down the
hill to visit his mother, had it not been for Geacles. Geacles saw everything, knew everything.
Still, where was the harm in stretching his legs a
bit? Mur sauntered forth, around the hill. He
passed above the tannery, now dark and quiet
but reeking with a hundred odors in conflict.
From behind him came a small noise. Mur looked
back, then stepped into the shadow of the chemical shed. He waited. A furtive sound. Footsteps:
hastening, pausing, hastening again. A figure
came past, peering ahead with mischievous intensity: Geacles.

Mur watched him sidle around the angle of
the tannery. Geacles worked on the principle
that what was bad for others was good for himself and hoped to gain advantage of some unspec-
ified sort by spying. So much was clear. Mur
stood quiet in the dark, not particularly surprised
nor even angry; it was what he expected of
Geacles . . . Not too far away was the meditation chamber where young Chilites gathered before entering the temple for nocturnal commu-
nion with Galexis. Mur slipped through the
shadows to a soaking vat. Holding his breath
against the stench, he prodded and pulled with a

turning prong and succeeded in lifting a hide. At a gingerly half trot he carried it up and around to the meditation chamber. Through the window came a mumble of voices: ". . . Galexis of a million beatific forms, individual but universal, for all but each alone, submissive but magnificent in your forward search; we avert our souls from sordid stuffs, the greases and taints, the First Order Palpabilities!"

Then voices a half octave lower in response: "Tonight, all will be well; tonight, all will be well."

Then the start of a new declamation: "Galexis of the myriad colors, the infinite graces—"

Through the open window Mur tossed the hide. A startled curse interrupted the declamation. Mur trotted back to his bay. Minutes later three of the young Chilites came to look into the chamber. Mur, in the recommended invocative posture, feigned sleep. At Geacles's bay a Chilite gave a low hoarse call, "One is gone; make search, make search! The Pure Boy Geacles!"

They ran back through the pale starlight and discovered Geacles lurking below the tannery. He protested innocence with every degree of fervor; he claimed the virtue of vigilance in following Pure Boy Mur whose erratic behavior had engaged his attention. In their outrage the Chilites paid no heed; one Pure Boy convenient to hand was better than another not demonstrably guilty. Geacles was treated to a thrashing, then forced to remove the hide and give the meditation chamber a ritual cleansing: a process occupying three nights and two days. Next, Geacles went before the Development Committee where he was asked a number of searching questions. He had now toiled three nights and two days without sleep;

in a half hysteria he babbled the first words that came into his head: a hysterical demonstration that impressed the Committee favorably, rather than otherwise. Geacles was basically good substance, they decided; his astonishing act must be ascribed to an ecstatic predisposition. Geacles received a cursory reprimand and was ordered to restrain his volatility.

During the examination Geacles identified Mur as the source of the mischief, to which information the commission presented faces of indifferent skepticism; nonetheless, they took note of the name. Geacles sensed something of the committee's mood and was heartened, though his skin crawled with detestation for Mur. Alternately giggling in jubilation and groaning in fury, he returned to the Pure Boy chambers where the scandal had been discussed from every possible aspect. In silence the Pure Boys watched Geacles as he crossed the chamber. He went to his bay and lay himself upon the pallet, too tired to sleep, his mind crawling with malice. Through slitted eyes he watched Mur, wondering how he would take revenge. Some way, somehow, by one means or another . . . Geacles fermented with emotion. His hate became so great that he began to shudder. He gave a small animal moan and quickly turned his back, lest others should notice his precious hate and use it for derision. Then it would be soiled and spoiled . . . A peculiar condition overcame Geacles, wherein his body slept but his mind seemed to remain awake. Time foreshortened; about ten minutes passed, or so he estimated; he turned to look around the chamber, and found that the suns had wheeled far across the sky. The hour was well past noon; Geacles

had missed his lunch: cause for new anguish! He
noticed Mur sitting on a bench at the open end of
the chamber. He held a copy of the Analytical
Catechism, but his attention was fixed across the
landscape. He seemed distraught. Geacles raised
his head, wondering what went on in Mur's mind.
Why did his fingers twitch, why did he frown so
intently? Mur gave a peculiar jerk, as if at a message from his subconscious. He rose to his feet
and, as oblivious as a somnambulist, departed the
chamber.

Geacles groaned in doubt and indecision. He
still ached with fatigue. But Mur's conduct was
not that of a Pure Boy. He heaved himself from
his couch and went to peer after Mur. Was he
off to tend his silk? Conceivably. But again—Mur's
gait was not that of a truly consecrated Pure Boy.
Geacles drew a deep breath. His curiosity had
only just brought him to grief, in circumstances
exactly similar. He dragged himself back to his
bay where he immersed himself in his own Analytical Catechism:

"Q: In how many guises may Galexis ap-
    pear?
"A: Galexis is as protean as the face of the
    ocean . . ."

A week passed. Geacles behaved with easy cor-
diality toward all; the Pure Boys treated him with
cautious reserve. Mur paid him no heed whatever. But Geacles gave a great deal of quiet attention to Mur. And one day while Geacles sat in his
bay memorizing Exclamations, Mur went to sit
on the bench at the open end of the chamber.
Geacles instantly became interested and over the

top of his book watched Mur's every move. Mur seemed to be talking to himself. Hmf, grunted Geacles to himself, he merely recited a litany or Exclamations. But why did his finger tap with so regular a beat on his knee? Peculiar. Geacles watched even more intently. Mur returned to his bay; Geacles instantly frowned down into his Exclamations. Shelving his Catechism, Mur went back to the front of the chamber. Here he paused a moment or two, looking out over the sweep of the landscape. After a single backward glance into the chamber, he set off along the hillside. Geacles instantly left his bay and went to look after Mur, who marched purposefully along the path to the north. Toward his plot of fiber-trees, thought Geacles with a sniff. Mur, or rather Faman Bougozonie, had always been assiduous with his trees. Still, why the backward glance into the chamber? Geacles rubbed his pale cheeks. Interesting, interesting. To learn he must look, with his round yellow-brown eyes; to look he must move himself within range of vision. After all, there was no reason why he should not tend his own silk; it had been sorely neglected over the last few weeks. Geacles disliked the routine of winding bobbins, weeding, propping branches, drawing down new strands; but now duty offered a pretext upon which he might follow Mur without fear of challenge.

Geacles set off along one of the paths that curved around the parched hillside. He tried to contrive a sedate and purposeful gait and simultaneously maintain stealth: no mean feat; had Mur been other than lost in his brooding, Geacles would have been forced to relinquish one or the other of his attitudes.

But Mur went unheeding down into the silk-tree brake, and Geacles, ducking and sidling, followed.

From the age of eight Mur had tended eighteen full-size trees, with over a hundred bobbins. He knew the angle of each twig, the cast of each leaf, the sap that each branch might be expected to provide. Each bobbin had its idiosyncrasy; in some, if the glass spring were wound too tightly, the ratchet would jam; others refused to turn unless tilted; a few worked flawlessly, and these Mur used under the highest beads.

Geacles watched from concealment while Mur made the rounds of his bobbins, winding the mechanisms, replacing full spools with empty ones, pinching suckers from the trunks. A dozen branches had gone dry; Mur cut into fresh shoots. The beads of sap oozed forth; Mur drew down filaments, which hardened at once into strands of silk. Mur attached the ends to bobbins, assured himself that the rotating spools drew down the strands at a steady rate. Geacles watched in glum disappointment; Mur's conduct was that of an industrious, innocent, and responsible Pure Boy.

Mur began to move at purposeful speed, as if he were anxious to finish. Geacles ducked back out of sight as Mur stepped forward to make a careful scrutiny of the hillside. Geacles grinned; Mur's conduct was no longer that of an innocent Pure Boy.

Mur set off downhill, moving so quickly that Geacles was hard put to follow. Mur reached the path that skirted the boundary behind Rhododendron Way and set off to the east. Geacles was now at something of a disadvantage. If he followed along the path, he must disclose himself. He darted through the berry patch, blundering into a nettle patch. Cursing and hissing, he took shelter among the rhododendrons. Mur was well along the patch, almost out of sight. Geacles followed crouching, dodging, running. He gained a spot where he could look along the path. Mur was nowhere to be seen. Geacles deliberated a moment, then pushed down into Rhododendron Way, highly questionable territory for a Pure Boy, not precisely tainted but still ground to be walked on gingerly. No Mur. Puzzled now, Geacles returned to the path. Where was Mur? Had he gone into one of the cottages? Geacles licked his lips in horror, trotted along the path toward the cottage of Eathre. He paused to listen: Eathre was entertaining a musician. But where was Mur? Geacles looked this way and that. Surely not in the cottage with his mother and the musician. Geacles walked past, angry and uncomfortable. In some unfathomable manner Mur had evaded him. . . . The music halted, then, after a few runs and arpeggios, began again. It seemed to be coming not from the cottage but the garden. Geacles crept close, peered through the foliage. He turned. Fleetly, soundlessly, bounding like a hare, Geacles ran up the hill toward the temple. Eathre, glancing from her window, saw him go.

Fifteen minutes passed. Down the hill on long point-footed strides came Great Male Osso, followed by two other Chilites, all three red-eyed from their galga-induced spasms. At the back came Geacles. The group marched down into Rhododendron Way.

At Eathre's cottage the group halted. The midday air was warm; the three suns rolled overhead, projecting triple images in the dust of the road. No sound could be heard but the drone of the spiral-bugs in the foliage and a far thumping from the tannery.

Standing well back from the door, Osso signaled to a nearby child. "Summon forth the woman Eathre."

The child timidly went around to the back of Eathre's cottage. A moment later the door opened; Eathre looked forth. She stood quietly, passive but alert.

Great Male Osso demanded, "The Pure Boy Faman Bougozonie—is he here?"

"He is not here."

"Where is he?"

"So I should guess, elsewhere."

"He was seen here not fifteen minutes ago."

Eathre had no comment to make. She waited in the doorway.

Osso spoke in a ponderous voice. "Woman, you would do well not to obstruct us."

Eathre smiled faintly. "Where do you see obstruction? Search as you will. The boy is not within; nor has he been, today or any other day since his rite."

Geacles darted behind the cottage where he signaled. The Chilities, clutching their robes to themselves, went to look. Geacles pointed in excitement. "He sat on yonder bench. The woman evades."

Osso spoke portentously: "Woman, is this true?"

"Why should he not sit there? The bench does him no taint."

"Are you a keen judge of this? Where is the boy?"

"I don't know."

Osso turned to Geacles. "Try the Pure Boy quarters. Fetch him here."

With great zeal Geacles sprang away, arms and legs pumping. He returned in five minutes, grinning and panting like a dog. "He is coming, he comes."

Mur stepped slowly forth into the road.

Osso stood back. Mur, wide-eyed and somewhat pale, asked, "Why did you wish to see me, soul-father?"

"I call to your attention," said Osso, "the sorry fact that you came here mother-milking and playing idle music."

"With utmost respect, soul-father, you have been misled."

"There is the witness!"

Mur looked toward Geacles. "He has not told the truth."

"Did you not sit on this bench, a woman's thing? Did you not take a musical instrument from this woman's hand? You are female-foul and not on good footing."

"The bench, soul-father, is from outside the under-temple. Notice, it stands away from the cottage, across the garden boundary. The khitan is my own property and was given me years ago by a man. Before my rite I took it into the temple and passed it through agapanthus smoke; you can still smell the reek. Since then, it has been kept in the play-hut I built with my own hands yonder; there it is now. I am guilty of no defilement whatever."

Osso looked blinking up at the sky while he gathered his thoughts. He was being made ridiculous by two Pure Boys. Faman Bougozonie with great cleverness had avoided any act of flagrant defilement, but this very cleverness indicated corruption. . . . Geacles Vonoble, while inaccurate in his assertions, had correctly diagnosed impurity. If anything was certain, it was that Faman Bougozonie's sophistries should not put truth and orthodoxy to rout. Osso said, "This seems a peculiar retreat for a Pure Boy, the yard behind his mother's cottage."

"It seemed as good as any other, soul-father, and here at least I would disturb no one while I meditated."

"Meditated?" croaked Osso. "Playing jigs and kestrels while the other Pure Boys performed devotions?"

"No, soul-father; the music helped fix my thoughts, exactly as you recommended."

"What? You claim that I recommended such an affair?"

"Yes, soul-father. You declared that you found the construction of imaginary knots helpful to your austerities and permitted that I employ musical tones to the same end."

Osso stood back. The other two Chilites and Geacles looked at him expectantly. Osso said, "I envisioned different tones, in a different environment. Your conduct stinks of secularity! And woman, what of you? Are you slack-witted? Surely you must know such conduct to be incorrect?"

"I hoped, Great Male, that the music would assist him in his future life."

Osso chuckled. "The mother of Pure Boy Chalres, the mother of Pure Boy Faman. What a pair! You shall spawn no more such prodigies. To the tannery." Osso swung around, pointed a finger at Mur. "As for you, we shall test the erudition you claim to have achieved."

"Soul-father, if you please, I only aspire to erudition!" cried Mur, but Osso already had turned away. Mur looked toward Eathre, who gave him a smiling shrug and went into the cottage. Mur whirled toward Geacles, but the Chilites stood in his way. "To the temple with you; did you not hear your soul-father?"

Mur marched up the path to the temple. He went to his bay. Geacles followed and went to his own alcove where he sat looking across the room at Mur.

An hour passed; a chime sounded. The Pure Boys trooped into the refectory. Mur hesitated, then turned a look back over the landscape, across road and cottages and off into the purple distances.

Geacles was watching. Mur heaved a sigh and went down the passage toward the refectory.

At the entrance stood the Chilite monstrator. He signaled Mur aside. "This way."

He led Mur around the temple to a disused under-chamber. He swung open an old timber door and signaled Mur to enter. Holding high a glow-bulb, the monstrator led the way along a passage rich with the reek of old galga fume into a large circular chamber at the very heart of the temple. The limestone walls were dank and gave off the odor of mold; the floor was dark brick. From the ceiling hung a single light globe. "What is this place?" Mur quavered.

"It is a place of solitary study where you will remain prior to your Repurification."

" 'Repurification'!" cried Mur. "But I am not defiled."

"Come, come," said the monstrator. "Why dissemble? Do you believe you can outwit your soul-father Osso, or myself for that matter? If you did not physically defile yourself, you committed a hundred acts of spiritual defilement." He waited, but Mur was silent. "Notice," the monstrator went on, "there are books on the table yonder: Doctrines and Exclamations, an Analytical Catechism. These will give you comfort and wise counsel."

Mur scowled around the chamber. "How long must I stay here?"

"A proper time. In the cabinet is food and drink; to the side is a sump. Now a final word: submit and all will be well. Do you hear?"

"Monstrator, I hear."

"Life is a choice of paths. Make sure you choose correctly because you may never return to choose again. Call for Galexis!"

The monstrator departed into the corridor. Mur looked after him, half of a mind to follow. . . . But he had been brought here to meditate; if he departed, he would incur something worse than Repurification.

He listened. Nothing but the secret murmur of underground places. He went to stand in the gap and peered down the corridor. Surely someone watched. Or an alarm or a trap had been set. If he tried to follow the monstrator, he might encounter something unpleasant. "Submit," the monstrator had told him. "Submit and all will be well."

Submission might well be the wisest course.

Soberly Mur turned away from the opening. He went to look at the table and, seating himself, examined the books. The Doctrines were hand-printed in purple ink on alternate sheets of red and green paper; they were inordinately difficult to read and contained many strange expressions. Nonetheless, thought Mur, it would be wise to study them carefully. The Exclamations, to be uttered during nocturnal worship, were not quite so important, adding only elegance, as they did, to the spasms.

Mur recalled that he had eaten no lunch and, jumping up, went to the cabinet. He found a dozen packets of dried berries: enough to nourish him for as many days, or even longer, were he frugal, as common sense dictated. Three dark green glass jugs held ample water. There was no cot or couch; he must sleep on the bench. He returned to the table, took up the Analytical Catechism, and began to read:

Q: How long have Chilites known Galexis?
A: Four thousand years ago the Great System was initiated by Hakcil, who was prompted to the use of galga by an overbearing and malodorous spouse.
Q: How many guises does Galexis assume?
A: Galexis is as protean as the face of the ocean and is at once singular to each and universal to all.
Q: Where was Galexis before the Chilites discovered the sacred herb?
A: Galexis, sempiternal and immanent, has given umbral revelation to men of all eras, but only the Chilites, by performing the Absolute Dichotomy, have made Galexis real.
Q: What is the Absolute Dichotomy?
A: It is that act of perception that, on designating Corporeal Female as dross and

taint, celebrates the Beatitude of Galexis.

Q: What is the purpose of the Holy Recep-
tacle?

A: In the dueness of time, a Perfection will
be yielded: the fruit of Galexis and the
males.

Q: What will be Perfection's Role and Destiny?

A: He shall take news of Galexis across the
worlds. Where he walks the females
shall cry woe . . .

Mur put down the catechism, which he found
unutterably boring. He noticed marks on the
table: dozens of marks. Names carved into the
wood, some worn by time, others comparatively
fresh. . . . What was this one? "Chalres Gargamet." Something cold gripped the pit of Mur's
stomach. Here they had brought Chalres. How
had he died? Mur rose slowly to his feet. He
stared around him. Were there other entrances?
He made a circuit of the room, testing the damp
limestone that everywhere seemed solid. He
slowly returned to the table and stood under the
lamp. His skin crawled as he considered the
bleak shape of his future. The Repurification rite
might well be more rigorous than the original
rite. The open door held a horrible fascination. It
indicated the way to the outdoors where Mur
dearly longed to be; on the other hand, it
threatened a terrible penalty. He thought of
Chalres, dead, broken, face down in the tannery
sump.

Desolation seeped over Mur's spirit. The light
cast a weird glare, illuminating the pitiful

scratchings on the table. He must submit.

Time passed: an hour. Mur listlessly chanted passages from the Catechism, words without meaning. He studied the Doctrine: Hakcil's Original Elucidations. The volume was old, dog-eared, a fixture of the chamber. Mold had blurred the writing; the pages adhered to each other. The purple characters blurred into the red and green pages. Mur put down the book and studied the doorway: so appealing and so baleful. He speculated. Suppose he were to run down the passage, so swiftly that his feet skimmed the ground. He might gain the open air by sheer audacity. No. It would not be done so easily. By some means he would be trapped. The timber door might be locked. For his insubordination he would meet Chalres's fate. This was the Chilite way. If he made ignoble and utter submission, abasing himself before soul-father Osso with fervent declarations of purity and disavowals of all and any mother-milking, past, present, and future, he could preserve his status as a Pure Boy.

Mur licked his lips. It was better than the sump. He bent over the Doctrine, committing whole paragraphs to memory, working till his head swam and his eyes smarted. On the fourth page mold obscured the characters across fully half a page; the fifth and sixth pages were likewise blotched. Mur peered at the pages in dismay. How could he learn the Elucidations when they were illegible? Osso would never accept any such glib excuse. "Why were you not prepared with your own copy of Hakcil? When I was a Pure Boy, it was my constant companion!" Or, "These pages are elementary. You should have known them long ago." On the other hand, reflected Mur, the marred volume offered a valid pretext for him to try the corridor. If someone were on guard, he could display the illegible pages and ask for an "Elucidations" in better condition. Mur half-rose to his feet. The corridor showed as a sinister dark rectangle.

Mur sat down once more. The time must be well into the night; no Chilite would be standing on guard, certainly! Nor any Pure Boy. Might there be an alarm of some sort? Mur thought the prospect unlikely. The Chilites would not care to be disturbed at their spasms.

The outer door had not been locked; perhaps the corridor was open! Mur licked his lips. More likely the passage held its own protection: a pitfall, a snare, a booby trap. A net or a cage might drop to imprison him. The way might be altered to lead into a cul-de-sac or a return loop with sand or mud on the floor to trace his prowling. Or the passage might lead to a brink and send him tumbling to his death.

Mur glanced furtively sidelong at the dark portal, which now seemed to have secret eyes of its own. He sighed and returned to the mildewed books. But he could not concentrate; absently, with a stone chip, he scratched his name on the table top with the others: in sad consternation he saw that he had carved "Gastel Etzwane." Another evidence of contumacy, should anyone see. He raised his hand to scratch it out but in sudden anger threw the stone chip into the corner. He glared defiantly at the name. This was himself; he was Gastel Etzwane; they could kill him a thousand times before he'd become anyone else! His small flare-up of defiance waned. The facts were as before. He must remain here in the study

chamber an unknown period, then face Repurification. Or, despite the cold crawling up and
down his back, he could test the passage.

Slowly he rose to his feet and crossed the
room, one furtive step at a time. He looked down
the passage as far as the overhead bulb cast a
glimmer—ten or fifteen feet. He looked back up
at the bulb; it hung ten feet over his head. He
stood the bench on the table and climbed up; the
bulb still hung three feet out of reach. Mur descended to the floor, awkward and lumpish as an
old man; once more he went to look into the dark
passage.

Beyond all reasonable doubt it was locked off—
or it held a trap. Mur tried to remember the way
of the passage. As the monstrator walked ahead,
he had held his light bulb high, revealing a
vaulted ceiling of dank stone. Mur had seen
neither cages nor dangling nets, though these
might easily have been arranged after his passage. The trip in such a case must be a thread
across the corridor, or perhaps an electrical contact, though the Chilites had small electrical ex-
pertise and in fact distrusted both electricity and
biomechanisms. The trap, if it existed, would be
simple and more than likely activated by a trip
close to the floor.

Mur's heart rose up in his mouth as he con-
templated the dark tunnel. It was the most important moment of his life. As Faman Bougozonie he could remain at the table to study
Catechism and the incomplete Elucidations; he
could become a fervent Chilite. As Gastel Etzwane he could grope along the passageway and
hope to reach the open night.

Chalres's pitiful soiled body rose up in front of

his eyes. Mur made a thin high-pitched sound of desperation. He had another vision: the face of his soul-father Osso; the high receding forehead with hair clinging in sparse locks, the intent, red-rimmed eyes carefully scrutinizing. Mur gave another thin whimper; dropping to his hands and knees, he crept into the dark.

The light went dim behind him. Mur began a careful investigation of the darkness, feeling out with great delicacy and caution for thread, string, rod, or trip-board. The passage, so he recalled, would turn first left, then right; he kept close to the left wall.

Darkness was complete. Mur tested the air as if searching for cobwebs. When nothing perceptible was evident, he felt the floor with equal care, probing every inch before he pulled himself forward.

Foot by painful foot he advanced, darkness pressing upon him like a palpable substance. He was too tense to feel fear; past and future were out of mind; there was only now, with grinding danger close at hand. With fingers like moth antennae he searched the darkness: on these fingers his life depended. To his left he lost contact with the wall; the first turn. He stopped short, feeling the walls on both sides, testing the joints of the stone blocks. He turned the corner, anxious to advance but reluctant to leave safe tested territory. He could still return to the study chamber. Ahead lay the area where danger most likely might be expected. With the most exquisite care he searched the darkness, feeling the air, the walls, the floor. Inch by inch, foot by foot he moved forward. His fingers felt a strange texture along the floor: a rasp, a grain, not so cold as stone. Wood. Wood on the floor. Mur felt for the joint between stone and wood. It ran across the passage at right angles to the walls. With his knees on the stone Mur reached ahead, feeling first for thread, then testing the floor, now wood. He discovered no thread; the wood seemed sound. He discovered no brinks, no lack of solidity. Laying flat on his face, Mur reached forward as far as his arms could stretch. He felt only wood. He wriggled ahead a few inches and felt again. Wood. He pounded down with his fist and thought to hear a hollow boom rather than the dullness of a plank on soil or mortar. Danger, danger. He inched forward. The floor began to tilt, elevating his feet. Hastily he retreated. The floor dropped back into place. The wooden section was pivoted near the center. Had he been walking, groping along the walls, he could not have recovered. Once past the balance point, with the back half of the trap rising into the air, he would have been gone, to fall toppling and sprawling through the darkness to whatever lay below. Mur lay quiet, his lips drawn back in a wolfish grin. He measured from stone to pivot-place: the length of his body, five feet. Ahead, after the pivot, was presumably another five feet of unsupported surface. Had he carried a light, he might have risked a running leap. But not in the dark. Suppose he miscalculated and jumped short. Mur's grin became so tight the muscles of his cheeks ached. He needed a plank, a ladder, something of the sort. He thought of the bench, back in the study chamber, which was six feet long. Rising to his feet, feeling along the wall he returned much faster than he had come. The chamber was quiet, almost somnolent. Mur took up the bench and carried it back into the dark passage, which now he knew so well. He reached the turn and, once again cautious, dropped to his hands and knees and dragged the bench beside him, upside down. He came to the wood section; bringing the bench past him, he thrust it ahead until he estimated that the near end rested over the pivot and the far end, hopefully, on solid stone. With the utmost care and precision he rested his weight on the bench, ready to scramble back at a quiver.

The bench held steady. Mur crossed and at the far end felt stone under his fingers. He grinned, this time in relief and pleasure.

He was not yet free of the passage. He proceeded as cautiously as before, and presently came to the second turn. A few yards ahead glimmered a wan bulb. It shone on a door: the old timber door giving upon the unused underroom. Heart in throat once more, Mur stepped forward. The door was locked—not so much to keep him in, he suspected, but to prevent some unwary Chilite or Pure Boy from blundering upon the trap.

Mur made a sad sound and went to look at the door. It was built of solid planks, doweled and glued, with hinges of sintered ironweb. The frame was wood, somewhat soft and rotten, thought Mur. He pushed against the door, bracing himself and thrusting with the trifling weight of his immature body. The door stood firm. Mur hurled himself at the door. He thought the latch creaked slightly. He battered himself again and again at the door, but other than causing a creaking of old wood he achieved nothing. Mur's body became bruised and sore, though the pain meant nothing to him. He stood back panting. He remembered

the bench and ran back down the passage, around
the turn, and slowly forward until he felt the end
of the bench. He dragged it across the trap-sec-
tion and carried it back to the door. Aiming it, he
ran forward and thrust the end against the latch.
The frame splintered. The door burst back, and
Mur was out into the under-room, echoing and
empty.

He placed the bench along one of the walls
where it would never be noticed. Closing the door,
he pressed the splintered wood into place. It
might well escape notice, and the Chilites would
have cause for perplexity!

A moment later he stepped out into the night
and looked up at the blazing Skiaffarilla. "I am
Gastel Etzwane," he muttered in exultation. "As
Gastel Etzwane I escaped the Chilites; as Gastel
Etzwane I have much to do."

He was not yet free and away. His escape
would be discovered in due course: perhaps in
the morning, at the latest within two or three
days. Osso could not call upon the Faceless Man,
but he might well send up into the Wildlands for
ahulph trackers. No trail was too old or too faint
for the ahulphs; they would follow until their
quarry mounted a wheeled vehicle, a boat, or a
balloon. Gastel Etzwane must once again use his
ingenuity. Osso would expect him to flee, to put
all possible distance between himself and Bashon.
Hence, if he remained close for a day, until the
ahulphs had cast about fruitlessly and had been
sent with a curse back to their master, he might
be able to go his way unhindered—wherever the
way might lie.

A hundred yards below and around the hill lay
the tannery, its sheds and outbuildings with doz-

ens of secure nooks and crannies. Gastel Etzwane
stood to the side of the portal, hidden in the
shadow, listening to the night sounds. He felt as
strange and subtle as a ghost. Above in the temple the Chilites lay in the galga smoke worship-
ing Galexis; their gasps of adoration were stifled
in the heavy darkness.

Gastel Etzwane stood several moments in the
shadows. He felt no urgency, no need for haste.
His first concern was the ahulphs, which almost
certainly would be called on to track him by
signs invisible to human senses. He slipped back
into the temple and presently found an old cloak,
that had been cast aside in a corner. Taking it to
the portal, he tore it in half. Throwing down first
one half on the stony ground, then the other, and
jumping forward, he made his way away from
the temple and down the slope, leaving neither
track nor scent for the ahulphs. Gastel Etzwane
laughed in quiet exultation as he reached the
first of the tannery outbuildings.

He took refuge under one of these sheds. Pil-
lowing his head on the torn cloak, he fell asleep.

Sasetta, Ezeletta, and Zael came dancing up
over the horizon, to shoot shifting beams of
colored light from the east. From the temple
sounded a throbbing chime, summoning the Pure
Boys to the temple kitchens where they must boil
up gruel for the Chilites' breakfast. Into the east-
ern courtyard came the Chilites themselves, haggard and red-eyed, their beards stinking of galga
smoke. They staggered to benches and sat looking drearily off into the wan sunlight, still somewhat bemused. The tannery women already had
taken bread and tea; they trudged forth for roll

call, some surly, others voluble. The task-mis-
tresses called out names for special assignments;
the women specified went off in various directions.
A select few, all matriarchs of the Sisterhood,*
sauntered to the chemical shed to compound
herbs and powders, dyes and astringents. Another group went to the vats to scrape, trim, soak,
steep, drain. Others worked new hides delivered
by the Wildland ahulphs: pelts of all the wilderness animals, ahulph hides as well. After sorting,
they were laid out on circular wooden tables,
where they were given a rough cleaning, trimmed
and shaped, then slid down a chute into a vat of
lye. To the cleaning tables Eathre had been assigned; she had been issued a brush, a glass knife,
a small, sharp spoon-scraper. Jatalie, the work-
mistress, stood over her, giving instructions.
Eathre worked quietly, hardly taking her eyes
from the work. She seemed apathetic. Etzwane's
hiding place was no more than a hundred feet
distant; he wriggled and squirmed to where he
could peer through a niche in the foundation;
upon seeing his mother, he could barely restrain
himself from calling out. His gentle mother in
such vulgar conditions! He lay biting his lips and
blinking. He could not even offer consolation!

From the direction of the temple came a small
commotion. Pure Boys ran out in excitement to
peer across the valley; Chilites appeared on the
upper terrace, talking in some agitation, pointing here and there. Etzwane guessed that his absence had been discovered somewhat earlier than
he had expected. He watched in a discordant

* The *Zoriani nac Thair nac Thairi*. In loose translation:
Female Agents of Desperate Deeds.

blend of dread and glee. Amusing to see the Chilites in such perturbation; horrifying as well! If he
were tracked down and captured . . . His flesh
crawled at the thought.

Shortly before noon he observed the arrival of
the ahulphs: two bucks with red adept ribbons
tied up and down the coarse black fur of their
crooked legs. Great Male Osso, standing austerely
on a pedestal, explained his needs in dadu*; the
ahulphs listened, laughing like foxes. Osso
dropped a shirt that Etzwane presumed to be one
of his own. The ahulphs seized the shirt in their
manlike hands, pressed it to the odor-detectors in
their feet, tossed it into the air in a display of the
raffish heedlessness that the Chilites found completely detestable. They went to Osso and gave
him vehement, waggish reassurance; Osso at last
made an impatient gesture. The ahulphs, after
looking this way and that for something worth
stealing, went to the Pure Boys' under-room.
Here, detecting Etzwane's scent, they leapt into
the air and called back to Osso in vast excitement.

The Pure Boys watched in horrified excitement,
as did Etzwane himself, for fear that some trace
of his odor might waft itself to the ahulphs.

The two cast about the temple, and Etzwane
was relieved when they crossed his trail and discovered nothing. Somewhat dampened, with ear-
flaps hanging dolefully low, they traced around
Eathre's old cottage, again without success. Rag-
ing at each other in ahulph fashion, snapping,
kicking out with the white talons concealed in
their soft black feet, swirling their fur in spiral

* Dadu: a language of finger signs and the syllables *da,
de, di, do, du.*

bristles, they returned to where Osso stood waiting and explained in dadu that the quarry had gone off upon wheels. Osso turned on his heel and stalked into the temple. The ahulphs ran south, back up Mirk Valley into the Hwan Wildlands.

Peering through his cranny, Etzwane watched the community take up its normal routine. The Pure Boys, disappointed at being deprived of a terrifying spectacle, resumed their duties. The tannery women worked stolidly at the vats, tubs, and tables. Chilites sat like thin white birds on benches along the upper terrace of the temple. Sunlight, tinted noontime lavender, struck down at white dust and parched soil.

The tannery workers went to the refectory. Etzwane directed urgencies toward his mother: *Come this way, come closer!* But Eathre moved off without turning her head. An hour later she returned to her table. Etzwane crawled back under the floor and worked up into the shed itself: a storage place for kegs of chemical, tools, and the like.

Etzwane found a lump of sal soda and, cautiously approaching the doorway, tossed the lump toward his mother. It dropped almost at her feet. She seemed not to notice. Then, as if suddenly interrupted from her thoughts, she glanced at the ground.

Etzwane tossed another lump. Eathre raised her head, looked blankly around the landscape, finally toward the shed. From the shadow Etzwane made a signal. Eathre frowned and looked away. Etzwane stared in puzzlement. Had she seen him? Why had she frowned?

Past the shed and into Etzwane's range of vision stalked Great Male Osso. He halted halfway

between the shed and the table where Eathre
worked. She seemed lost in another dimension of
consciousness.

Osso signaled the task-mistress and muttered a
few words. The woman went to Eathre, who without comment or surprise left her work and walked
toward Osso. He made a peremptory signal to
halt her while she was still fifteen feet distant
and spoke in a low burning tone. Etzwane could
not distinguish his words nor Eathre's calm responses. Osso jerked back and turned on his heel.
He stalked back past the shed, so close that had
Etzwane reached forth, he might have touched
the cold face.

Eathre did not instantly return to her work. As
if pondering Osso's words, she wandered over to
the shed and stood by the door.

"Mur, are you there?"

"Yes, mother. I am here."

"You must leave Bashon. Go tonight, as soon
as the sun goes down."

"Can you come with me? Mother, please come."

"No. Osso holds my indenture. The Faceless
Man would take my head."

"I will find the Faceless Man," declared Etzwane fervently. "I will tell him of the bad
things here. He will take Osso's head."

Eathre smiled. "Don't be too sure. Osso obeys
canton law—only too well."

"If I go, Osso will abuse you! He'll make you
work at all the hardest jobs."

"It is all the same. The days come and go. I am
glad you are leaving; it is what I wanted for you,
but I must stay and help Delamber through her
birth-times."

"But soul-father Osso may punish you, and all on my account!"

"No, he will not dare; the women are able to protect themselves, as I have only just put forward to your soul-father.* I must return to my work. After dark go forth. Since you wear no torc, be careful of the work-jobbers, especially in Durrume and Cansume and in Seamus as well, where they will put you into a balloon-gang. When you become of age, get a musician's torc; then you may travel without hindrance. Do not go to the old house, nor to Delamber's. Do not go for the khitan. I have a few coins put aside, but I can't get them for you now. I will not see you again."

"Yes you will, you will!" cried Etzwane. "I'll petition the Faceless Man, and he'll let you go with me."

Eathre smiled wistfully. "Not while Osso holds my identure. Good-by, Mur." She went back to the work table. Etzwane retreated into the shed. He did not watch his mother.

The day waned; the women trooped off to their

---

* Eathre alluded to the *Zoriani nac Thair nac Thairi*, which derived power from its ability to defile the temple or any particular Chilite. There were six degrees of defilement, the first being a touch of a female finger, the sixth a drenching with a bucketful of unmentionable substances. The Sister, or Sisters, who executed the defilements were volunteers, usually old, sick, and quite willing to end their lives dramatically by poison wads ingested immediately after achieving their goals.

Defilement impelled the Chilites to a month-long ritual of the most onerous Purification during which no galga was burnt; if the ecstatic trance were attempted previous to complete Purification, Galexis Achiliadnid appeared in horrid guise. During the period of Purification the Chilites became surly and restless. The Pure Boys were often victimized in one fashion or another.

dormitories. When darkness came, Etzwane emerged from the shed and stole off downhill.

Despite Eathre's warning he went down to the old cottage on Rhododendron Way, already occupied by another woman. He slipped to the rear, found the khitan, and went off through the shadows, down the road. He traveled west, toward Garwiy, where the Faceless Man lived—or so went the rumor.

Chapter 4

Shant, an irregular oblong thirteen hundred miles long and six hundred miles wide, was separated from the dark bulk of Caraz by a hundred miles of water: the Straits of Pagane flowing between the Green Ocean and the Purple Ocean. South across the Great Salt Bog, Palasedra hung down between the Purple Ocean and the Blue Ocean like a three-fingered hand or an udder with three teats.

A thousand miles east of Shant appeared the first islands of the Beljamar, a vast archipelago dividing the Green Ocean from the Blue Ocean. The population of Caraz was unknown; there were relatively few Palasedrans; the Beljamar supported a few scanty blotches of oceanic nomads; most of Durdane's population inhabited the sixty-two cantons of Shant, in loose confederation under the rule of the Faceless Man.

The cantons of Shant were alike only in their mutual distrust. Each regarded as Universal Principle its own customs, costumes, jargon, and mannerisms and considered all else eccentricity.

The impersonal, unqualified rule of the Anome —in popular usage, the Faceless Man—exactly suited the xenophobic folk of the cantons. Governmental apparatus was simple; the Anome made few financial demands; the laws enforced, for the most part, were those formulated by the cantons themselves. The Anome's justice might be merci-

less and abrupt, but it was evenhanded and adhered to a simple principle, clear to all: *He who
breaks the law dies*. The Faceless Man's authority derived from the torc, a band of flexite
coded in various shades of purple, dark scarlet or
maroon, blue, green, gray, and rarely, brown.*

The torc contained a strand of explosive;
dexax, which the Faceless Man, if necessary,
could detonate by means of a coded radiation. An
attempt to remove the torc worked to the same
effect. Usually, when a person lost his head, the
cause was well known: he had broken the laws
of his canton. On rare occasions, detonation might
take a person's head for reasons mysterious and
inscrutable, whereupon, folk would move with
great care and diffidence lest they, too, excite
the unpredictable wrath of the Faceless Man.

No area of Shant was too remote; from Ilwiy
to the Straits of Pagane detonations occurred and
felons lost their heads. It was known that the
Anome employed deputies, somewhat tartly

* By the usual Shant symbology blue, green, purple, and
gray carried optimistic attributes. Browns were unfavorable, tragic, elegant, authoritative, according to con-
text. Yellow was the hue of death. Red, signifying invisibility, was used to paint objects meant to be ignored.
Thieves wore red caps. White indicated mystery, chastity,
poverty, anger, dependent on circumstances. Colors in
combination changed significance.

In connection with color symbolism, the ideograms of
Canton Surrume might be mentioned. Originally each
word was represented by color strokes in correct symbolic combination; the scribe wrote with as many as
seven brushes in his fist. In due course a secondary system came into effect, employing monochromatic dots at
various heights, indicative of color, that in turn evolved
into a jointed line tracing the position of the color indica-
tors, and at last the sign for each word became a cursive
ideogram from which all reference to color had been lost.

known as Benevolences, who subserved the
Anome's will.

Garwiy, where the Faceless Man made his
headquarters, was the largest city of Shant, the
industrial node of all Durdane. Along the Jardeen
River and in the district known as Shranke on the
Jardeen Estuary were a hundred glassworks,
foundries and machine shops, biomechanical fab-
ricating plants, bioelectric works where the or-
ganic monomolecules of Canton Fenesq were
stranded into null-ohm conductors, bonded to
semi-living filters, valves, and switches, to produce fragile, temperamental, and highly expensive
electronic gear. Bio-engineers commanded high
prestige; at the opposite end of the social scale
were the musicians, who nevertheless excited
pangs of romantic envy in the settled folk of
Shant. Music, like language and color symbology,
transcended the canton boundaries, affecting the
entire population.*

In Canton Amaze a thousand, two thousand
musicians took part in the annual seiach: a vast
wash of sound swelling and subsiding like wind,
or surf, with occasional tides, vague and indis-
tinct, of clear little waif-bells. More general was
the music played by wandering troupes: jigs and
wind-ups; set-pieces and sonatas; shararas, sara-
bands, ballads, caprices, quick-steps. A druithine
might accompany such a troupe; more often he
wandered alone, playing as he fancied. Lesser
folk might sing words or chant poetry; the druithine played only music, to express his total experience, all his joy and grief. Such a person had
been Etzwane's blood-father, the great Dystar.

* A notable exception: the Chilites of Canton Bastern.

Etzwane had never credited the account of Dystar's death as related by Feld Maijesto; in his childhood daydreams Etzwane had seen himself wandering the roads of Shant, taking his khitan to fests and gatherings until at last the two met; from here the daydream went in various directions. Sometimes Dystar wept to hear music so lovely; when Etzwane identified himself, Dystar's wonder exceeded all bounds. Sometimes Dystar and the indomitable youth found themselves opposed in a battle of music; in his mind Etzwane heard the glorious tunes, the rhythms and counter-rhythms, the clink of the jingle-bar, the gratifying rasp of the scratch-box.

The daydreams at last had taken on a ghost of substance. Khitan slung over his narrow back, Etzwane trudged the roads of Shant, and all his future lay before him.

Unless he were captured and taken back to Bastern.

It was not beyond possibility that Osso would suspect the true state of affairs and call in the ahulphs once again. The thought put spring into Etzwane's steps. He jogged along at his best speed, slowing to a walk only when his lungs began to labor. Rhododendron Way lay far behind; he journeyed under the stars, with the great black hulk of the Hwan rising to his left.

The night wore on. Etzwane, no longer jogging, walked as fast as his aching legs would carry him. The road climbed a hill, rounded a spur. Behind spread a starlit landscape, gray and black, with a few far lights Etzwane could not identify.

He sat on a stone to rest and looked westward into Canton Seamus, which he had never seen be-

fore, though from men who passed along Rhododendron Way he knew something of the folk
and their habits. They were stocky, ruddy-blond,
and quick tempered; they brewed beer and dis-
tilled poteen, which men, women, and children
alike consumed without apparent effect. The men
wore suits of good brown cloth, straw hats, gold
rings in their ears; the women, who were stout
and boisterous, dressed in long pleated gowns of
brown and black and wore combs of aventurine
quartz in their hair. They never espoused men
larger than themselves; in the event that fisticuffs
took place after an evening at the tavern, the hus-
bands held no physical advantage.

The North Spur of the balloon-way passed
through Seamus, connecting Oswiy on the north
coast with the Great Transverse Line; the road
Etzwane followed met the balloon-way at Carbade. As he looked off to the west, over the country he planned to travel, he fancied to see far
away a red glimmer moving slowly across the sky.
If his eyes were not at fault, the light marked the
course of the balloon-way—though the time was
late and the wind was still. He thought of his
mother's warning against the work-jobbers; alone,
without a torc, he had no identity, he had claims
to no one's protection, and whoever so chose
could do as they liked with him. The work-jobbers
would clamp a torc and an indenture upon him,
ship him off to a balloon-gang. In the morning he
would contrive a torc of withe or bark or leather,
which would help him evade attention.

The time was late, and the night was still. So
still that as he sat quietly he thought to hear coming down from the Wildlands a far, faint howling.
Etzwane huddled down upon the stone, feeling

clammy and cool. The ahulphs were at one of
their macabre revelries, which came on them like
a madness; in some remote valley of the Hwan
they danced and howled around a fire.

The thought of ahulphs urged him to his feet.
When sure of a trail, they moved swiftly; he was
not yet beyond their reach.

He found that his legs had become stiff, and
his feet ached. He should never have seated himself to rest. As fast as he was able, he limped on
down the road into Seamus.

An hour before dawn he passed a village: a
dozen cottages around a small neat square paved
with slabs of slate. To the rear stood silos, a warehouse, and the bulbous tanks of a small brewery.
A three-story building beside the road was evidently an inn. Folk were already astir in the cook
shed to the rear; Etzwane saw the blink of a fire.
Beside the inn waited three large vans loaded
with fresh white butts and tubs of Shimrod Forest
larch destined for one or another of the distil-
leries. From the stable behind the inn a groom
was bringing draft animals: bullocks derived
from terrestrial beef stock, placid and depend-
able but slow.* Etzwane dodged past, hoping not
to be seen in the predawn murk.

The road ahead crossed a flat waste strewn
with rocks. No shelter was visible, nor any plantation from which he might have gleaned a bite or
two of nourishment. His spirits dropped to their
lowest ebb; he felt as if he could walk no more;

---

* The fragmentation of Shant into cantons can be at-
tributed both to the quality of the original settlers and the
lack of metal for efficient engines.

his throat was parched, and his stomach ached
with hunger. Only fear of the ahulph restrained
him from seeking a hidden spot among the rocks
in which to make himself a bed of dry leaves. Finally fatigue overcame the fear. He could walk
no longer. He stumbled to a spot behind a ledge
of rotten shale. Wrapping himself in his robe, he
lay down to rest. He lapsed into a numb daze,
something other than sleep.

A grating, grumbling sound aroused him: the
passage of the vans. The suns were an hour into
the sky; though he had not slept, or thought he
had not slept, daylight had come without his notice.

The vans passed by and rumbled away into
the west. Etzwane jumped up to look after them,
thinking that here was an opportunity to confuse
the ahulphs. The teamsters rode on the forward
benches and could not see to the rear. Etzwane
ran to catch up. He swung himself aboard the
last van and sat with his feet hanging over the
bed. After a few moments he drew himself farther back into a convenient crevice. He intended
to ride only a mile or two, then jump down, but
so convenient and comfortable was his seat, so
restful and secure seemed the dark nook, that he
became drowsy and fell asleep.

Etzwane awoke and blinked out from his
cranny at a pair of unrecognizable rectangles,
one impinged on the other. The first blazed lav-
dender-white; the second was a panel of striated
dark green. Etzwane's mind moved sluggishly.
What was this odd scene? He crawled slowly to
the back of the van, his mind still fuzzy. The
white was the wall of a whitewashed building in

the full glare of noon sunlight. The dark green panel was the side of a van thrust across his field of vision. Etzwane remembered where he was. He had been asleep; the cessation of motion had wakened him. How far had he come? Probably to Carbade, in Seamus. Not the best place to be if the oddments of information he had picked up along Rhododendron Way were to be believed. The folk of Seamus reputedly gave nothing and took whatever might be had. Etzwane climbed stiffly from the van. Best to be on his way before he was discovered. No more fear of the ahulphs, at any rate.

From not too far away came the sound of voices. Etzwane slipped around the van, confronting a black-bearded man with hollow white cheeks and round blue eyes. He wore a teamster's black canvas trousers, a dirty white vest with wooden buttons; he stood with legs apart, hands held up in surprise. He seemed pleased rather than angry. "And what have we here in this young bandit? So this is how they train them, to raid the cargo hardly before the wheels come to a stop. And not even a torc around his neck."

Etzwane spoke in a tremulous voice, that he tried to hold grave and earnest. "I stole nothing, sir; I rode only a short way in the van."

"That's theft of transportation," declared the teamster. "You admit the fact yourself. Well, then, come along."

Etzwane shrank back. "Come along where?"

"Where you'll learn a useful trade. I'm doing you a favor."

"I have a trade!" cried Etzwane. "I'm a musician! See! Here is my khitan!"

"You're nothing without your torc. Come along."

Etzwane tried to dodge away; the teamster caught him by the gown. Etzwane kicked and struggled; the teamster cuffed him, then held him off. "Do you want worse? Mind your manners!" He pulled at the khitan; the instrument fell to the ground where the neck snapped away from the box.

Etzwane gave a stifled cry and stared down at the tangle of wood and string. The teamster seized his arm and marched him into the depot to a table where four men sat at a gaming board. Three were teamsters; the fourth was a Seam, the conical straw hat pushed up from his round red face.

"A vagabond in my van," said Etzwane's captor. "Looks to be bright and lively; no torc, notice; what should I do to help him?"

The four gave Etzwane a silent inspection.

One of the teamsters grunted and turned back to the dice. "Let the lad go his way. He doesn't want your help."

"Ah, but you're wrong! Every citizen of the realm must toil; ask the job-broker here. What do you say, job-broker?"

The Seam leaned back in his chair, pushed his hat back at a precarious angle. "He's undersized; he looks unruly. Still, I suppose I can get him a post, perhaps up at Angwin. Twenty florins?"

"For the sake of quick business—done."

The Seam rose ponderously to his feet. He signaled to Etzwane. "Come along."

Etzwane was confined in a closet for the better

part of a day, then marched to a wagon and conveyed a mile south of Carbade to the balloon-way
depot. Half an hour later the southbound balloon
Misran appeared, wind on a broad reach, the dolly
singing up the slot. Observing the semaphore,
the wind-tender eased his forward cables, allow-
ing the *Misran* to fall broadside to the wind and
lose way. A quarter mile down the slot from the
depot the tackle-man hooked a drag to the dolly,
brought it to a halt, pinned the after trucks with
an anchor-bolt. The spreader-bar was detached;
the balloon-guys were slipped into snatch-blocks
on the front trucks; now the Judas dolly was
hauled south along the slot, pulling the balloon to
the ground.

Etzwane was taken to the gondola and put into
the charge of the wind-tender. The Judas-dolly
was rolled back along the track and engaged
with the spreader-bar, the balloon rising once
more to its running altitude. The anchor-pin was
removed from the after trucks. Front trucks,
thirty-foot spreader-bar, and after trucks con-
stituted the working-dolly; the *Misran* once more
rode free. The wind-tender winched in the forward guys, warping the balloon across the wind;
off and away up the slot sang the dolly, gathering
speed, and Carbade was left behind.*

---

* The typical balloon, carrying four to eight passengers
and a wind-tender, was a semiflexible slab one unit of
dimension wide, eight units long, four units high. The
skeleton might be bamboo, tempered glass tubing, or rods
of cemented glass fiber. The membrane was the dorsal
skin of a gigantic coelenterate, nurtured and forced until
it completely filled a large shallow tank, whereupon the
skin was lifted and cured. Hydrogen provided buoyancy.
  The slots in which the dollies ran were precast members
of concrete reinforced with glass fiber, attached to foun-

For Etzwane, the world of his daydreams was gone and lost irrevocably, like last year's flowers. He knew something of the balloon-way work-gangs; their lots were drudgery and compulsion. Technically free men, in practice they were seldom able to pay off their indentures. The condition of Etzwane was even worse; without a torc he had no status; he could appeal to no one; the work-master could set any value he chose on Etzwane's indenture. Once clamped with a torc, the Faceless Man would enforce the terms of his contract. Foreboding lay like a stone in his stomach; he felt numb and confused.

Deep inside his mind a voice began to yell. He would run away. He had escaped the Chilites; he would evade the work-gang. What had his mother told him? "Defeat adversities rather than accept them." Never would he let himself be victimized; after they clamped on his torc, he would win his way to Garwiy and there make a case to the Faceless Man: both for himself and his mother. He

---

dation-sleepers. The usual dolly consisted of two sets of trucks separated by a truss thirty feet long, at the ends of which the guys were attached. The wind-tender used trimming winches to shorten or lengthen bow and stern lines, thus controlling wind-aspect, and the canting winch, to alter the shape of the bridles at bow and stern and thus control the angle of heel.

Under optimum circumstances velocity reached sixty or seventy miles an hour. The routes made purposeful use of prevailing winds; where the route consistently encountered adverse winds or calm, motive power was applied to the dollies at ground level by an endless cable driven by water wheels or a work-gang at a windlass; by a gravity-cart loaded with stone; by teams of pacers. Balloons passed each other at sidings or traded dollies.

Where the route crossed gorges, as at Angwin Junction, or met otherwise unfavorable terrain, a cable of ironweb strands formed a link in the slot.

would ask a terrible punishment for the teamster
who broke his khitan; he had neglected to notice
the teamster's torc, but never would he forget the
pale, black-bearded face!

Stimulated by his hate and his resolve, he
began to take an interest in the balloon and the
landscape: low rolling hills rippling with ripe
barley, cylindrical stone farm places, round
grain towers, and, at intervals, the breweries,
with their curious bulging tanks.

During the middle afternoon the wind shifted
forward; the wind-tender winched in his forward
guy, to close-haul the balloon; driven closer to the
ground, he canted the bridles to provide lift, to
raise the *Misran* into a clear stream of air.

The rolling barley fields gave way to rocky hills
splotched with thickets of blue and dark orange
fester-shrub, from which the ancient ahulphs had
cut their weapons. To the south rose the Hwan,
the great central spine of Shant, across which
ran the Great Transverse Route. Late in the afternoon the *Misran* rushed up the last steep ten
miles of slot and reached Angwin North Station
where a work-gang shifted the guys to a shackle
on a mile-long endless cable suspended across a
gorge. The work-gang turned a windlass, the
Misran was guided sedately up to Angwin Junction where the North Spur joined the Great Transverse Route. The guys were shifted to another
endless loop, reaching across an even more
stupendous gorge to Angwin proper, and here the
Misran descended. The wind-tender took Etzwane
to the Angwin superintendent, who at first grumbled. "What kind of whiffets and sad bantlings are
they sending me now? Where can I use him? He

lacks weight to push a windlass; also, I don't like the look in his eye."

The wind-tender shrugged and glanced down at Etzwane. "He's a bit under the usual standard, but that's no business of mine. If you don't want him, I'll take him back down to Pertzel."

"Hmmf. Not so fast. What's his price?"

"Pertzel wants two hundred."

"For a creature like that? I'll give a hundred."

"That's not my instructions."

"Instructions be damned. Pertzel's using us both for fools. Leave the creature here. If Pertzel won't take a hundred, pick him up on your next trip. Meanwhile, I'll hold off his torc."

"A hundred is cheap. He'll grow; he's nimble; he can switch as many shackles as can a man."

"This I realize. He'll go across to Junction, and I'll bring the top man over here for the windlass."

The wind-tender laughed. "So you're getting a windlass-man for the price of a hundred-florin boy?"

The superintendent grinned. "Don't tell Pertzel that."

"Not I. It's between the two of you."

"Good. Ride him back to Junction; I'll flash over a message." He frowned down at Etzwane. "What's expected of you, boy, is brisk, accurate work. Do your stint and the balloon-way is not so bad. If you shirk or perform, you'll find me harsh as hackle-bush. . . ."

Etzwane rode back across the gorge to Angwin Junction. The *Misran* was hauled down by a hand-winch, a blond stocky youth not much older than Etzwane turning the crank.

Etzwane was put down; the *Misran* rose once

more into the gathering dusk and was hauled down over the gorge to North Station, on the North Spur.

The blond youth took Etzwane into a low stone shed where two young men sat at a table eating a supper of broad-beans and tea. The blond youth announced: "Here's the new hand. What's your name, lad?"

"I am Gastel Etzwane."

"Gastel Etzwane it is. I am Finnerack; yonder is Ishiel the Mountain Poet, and he with the long face is Dickon. Will you eat? Our fare is not the best: beans and bread and tea, but it's better than going hungry."

Etzwane took a plate of beans, which were barely warm. Finnerack jerked his thumb to the east. "Old Dagbolt rations our fuel, not to mention our water, provisions, and everything else worth using."

Dickon spoke in a surly voice: "Now I'll have to go grind windlass under Dagbolt's very nose. No talk, no chaffer; quiet, orderly work, that's Dagbolt for you. Here at least a man can spit in any direction he chooses."

"It's the same for all of us," said Ishiel. "In a year or two they'll bring me across, then it will be Finnerack's turn. And in the course of five or six years Gastel Etzwane will make the change, and we'll be reunited."

"Not if I can avoid it," said Dickon. "I'll put in for slot-cleaning duty and at least be on the move. If Dagbolt turns me down, I'll become the premier gambler of the Junction. Never fear, lads, I'll be out of my indenture before ten years have passed."

"My good wishes," remarked Finnerack. "You've

won all my money; I hope you get the service of it."

In the morning Finnerack instructed Etzwane in his duties. He would stand shifts in turn with Finnerack and Ishiel. When a balloon passed along the Great Transverse Route, he must ease the clamp and shackle around the idler sheave. When a balloon came up the North Spur, or returned, the man on duty, using a claw-lever chained to the floor, hooked into the guys and switched the balloon from one cable to the other. As the youngest member of the crew, Etzwane was also required to oil the sheaves, keep the hut swept out, and boil the morning gruel. The work was neither arduous nor complicated; the crew had ample leisure, which they spent crocheting fancy vests for sale in the town and gambling with the proceeds to earn enough to pay off their indenture. Finnerack told Etzwane, "Over at Angwin, Dagbolt forbids gambling. He says he wants to stop the fights. Bah. From time to time some lucky chap wins enough to buy himself free, and that's the last thing Dagbolt wants."

Etzwane looked around the station. They stood on a bleak windswept ledge fifty yards across, directly below the stupendous mass of Mount Mish and between two gorges. Etzwane asked, "How long have you been here?"

"Two years," said Finnerack. "Dickon has been here eight."

Etzwane studied Mount Mish and was daunted: impossible to scale the crag that beetled over the station. The precipices that descended into the gorges were no less baleful. Finnerack gave a sad, knowing laugh. "You'd like to find a way down?"

"Yes, I would."

Finnerack showed neither surprise nor disapproval. "Now's the time, before they clamp on your torc. Don't think I haven't considered it, torc and all."

At the edge of the precipice they looked down and off across a gulf of air. "I've stood here by the hour," said Finnerack wistfully, "tracing how I'd climb down to the valley. From here down to that nose of red granite a person would need a length of rope, or he might scramble down that fissure, had he the nerve. Then he'd have to work himself across the face of that scarp—it looks worse than it is, I dare say. From there to that tumble of scree should not be impossible, and only hard work thereafter down to the valley floor. But then what? It's a hundred miles to a village, with no food nor water. And do you know what you'd find along the way?"

"Wild ahulph."

"I wasn't thinking of ahulph, but you'd find them, too, the wicked Phag brood." Finnerack searched the valley floor. "I saw one just the other day." He pointed. "Look! By that needle of black rock. I think there's a cave or a shelter there. It's where I saw the other."

Etzwane looked and thought to see a stir of movement. "What is it?"

"A Roguskhoi. Do you know what that is?"

"It's a kind of mountain savage that can't be controlled except by its yearning for strong drink."

"Great womanizers, as well. I've never seen one close at hand, and I hope I never do. What if they took it into their heads to climb up here? They'd chop us to bits!"

"Much to Dagbolt's horror," suggested Etzwane.

"Too right! He'd have to buy in three new indentures. He'd rather we'd die of overwork or old age."

Etzwane looked wistfully down the valley. "I had planned to be a musician. . . . Does anyone ever earn enough to buy off their indentures?"

"Dagbolt does his best to prevent it," said Finnerack. "He operates a commissary where he sells Seam beer, fruit, sweetmeats, and the like. When the men gamble, it always seems to be one of the career ratings who wins the money, and no one knows how they achieve such luck. One way or another, it's not all so bad. Perhaps I'll make a career myself. There are always jobs opening up below—on the windlass or as a slot-cleaner or motive man. If you learn electrics, you might get into communications. As for me, I'd like to be a wind-tender. Think of it!" Finnerack flung back his head, looked around the sky. "Up in the balloon, running the winches, with the dolly skirring along the slot below. There's sheer fun! And one day it's Pagane and Amaze, the next Garwiy, then off over the Great Transverse Route to Pelmonte and Whearn and the Blue Ocean."

"I suppose it's not a bad life," said Etzwane dubiously. "Still—" he could not bring himself to finish.

Finnerack shrugged. "Until they torc you, you're free to run off. Be sure I won't stop you, or Ishiel. In fact we'll lower you down the cliff. But it's terrible country, and you'd be going to your death. Still—were I you, without my torc, perhaps I'd try." He raised his head as a horn sounded. "Come along; a balloon is crossing over from Angwin."

They returned to the station. The shift was technically Etzwane's; Finnerack was standing by to break him in. The approaching balloon hung aslant the sky, lurching and bobbing as the cable drew it against the wind. The guys, fore and aft, were shackled to an iron ring, which in turn was chained to a grip on the drive-line. The ring bore a black marker, indicating that it must be switched down the North Spur. The grip entered the sheave and passed halfway around the circumference. Finnerack pushed an electric signal to the windlass chief at Angwin and threw a brake that halted the drive-line. He hooked the claw-lever into the ring, worked the arm to pull down the ring and loosen the grip. Etzwane transferred the grip to the North Spur line; Finnerack disengaged the lever-jack; the balloon now hung on the North Spur drive-line. Finnerack pushed the electric signal to the windlass at North Station; the drive-line tautened, the balloon drifted away on the south wind.

Half an hour later another balloon arrived from the east, lurching and straining to the breeze blowing down from Mount Mish. The grip passed across the idler sheave without attention from Finnerack or Etzwane; the balloon continued across the gorge to Anwin, thence on toward Garwiy.

Not long after, another balloon came in from the west, destined as before to the North Spur. Etzwane said to Finnerack, "This time let me do the whole transfer. You stand to the side and watch that I do everything correctly."

"Just as you like," said Finnerack. "I must say you're very keen."

"Yes," said Etzwane. "I'm very keen indeed. I plan to take your advice."

"Indeed? And make a balloon-way career?"

"I plan to give the matter thought," said Etzwane. "As you have remarked, I am not yet clamped and not yet committed."

"Tell that to Dagbolt," said Finnerack. "Here comes the grip; be handy with the signal and the brake."

The grip entered the sheave; as it reached the circumference, Etzwane pressed the signal and braked the wheel.

"Quite right," said Finnerack.

Etzwane brought up the claw-jack, hooked it into the ring, drew down slack, and detached the grip.

"Exactly right," said Finnerack. "You've learned the knack, no question of it."

Etzwane caught the grip on the edge of the sheave, released the lever-jack, shook away the hook. He stepped up into the ring and kicked free the grip. Finnerack stared in bewilderment. "What are you doing?" he gasped. "You've set free the balloon!"

"Exactly," called Etzwane. "Give my regards to Dagbolt. Good-by, Finnerack."

The balloon swept him away on the wind from Mount Mish, while Finnerack watched openmouthed from below. Etzwane perched with one foot in the ring and, clutching the guy lines, waved his hand; Finnerack, standing foreshortened with head turned back, raised his arm in dubious farewell. Etzwane felt a pang of regret; he had never met anyone he liked so well as Finnerack. Someday they might meet again . . .

In the balloon the wind-tender realized that something had gone amiss but knew no remedy for the situation. "Attention all," he cried out to the passengers. "The guys have slipped; we are floating free in a northwest direction, which will take us safely across the Wildlands. There is no danger! Everyone please remain calm. When we approach a settled community, I will valve gas and lower us to the ground. For the unavoidable change of schedule I extend the official apologies of the balloon-way."

Chapter 5

The balloon floated down from the Hwan in the halcyon quiet of the upper air. Etzwane rode surrounded by lavender-white radiance; so unreal and peaceful were the circumstances, he felt no fear. Underneath passed the great forests of Canton Trestevan: parasol darabas, dark maroon and purple, soft-seeming as feather dusters, returning ripples of wincing greenish bronze to the touch of the wind. In the dank lower valleys stood redwoods, hoary giants five hundred feet tall, half as old as the coming of the human race. Lower still, along the piedmont, were hangman trees, black oaks and green elms, the unique syndic trees whose seeds sprouted legs and poisonous pincers. After walking to a satisfactory location, each seed roved within a ten-foot circle, poisoning all competing vegetation, then dug a hole and buried itself.

The forests persisted into Canton Sable, then gave way to a region of small farms and a thousand small ponds where crayfish, eels, whiteworm, a dozen other varieties of water-food were produced, packed, frozen, and shipped to the metropolitan markets of Garwiy, Brassei, Maschein. The villages were tiny toys exuding minuscule wisps of smoke; along the roads moved infinitesimal wagons and traps drawn by insect-size bullocks and pacers. Etzwane would have enjoyed the landscape, had he been comfortable.

He rode with first one foot in the ring, then the other, then one foot on top of the other. He tried to sit in the angle between the two guy lines, but the cables cut into his hips. His perch became more uncomfortable by the minute. His feet were knobs of pain; his arms and shoulders ached from the strain of clinging to the guys. Still, his exhilaration persisted; he had no fault to find with circumstances.

The wind had died to a murmur; the balloon drifted with great deliberation into Canton Frill, a green, dark blue, brown, white and purple checkerboard of fields and orchards. A meandering river, the Lurne, was a casual insult of nature to the human geometry of hedges and roads; ten miles to the west the river passed through a market town, built in the typical Frillish style: tobacco-brown panels of pressed gum-leaves between posts of polished iban, rising two or even three stories. Above the town rose a forest of poles, flying good-luck banners, prayer-flags, secret omens, tender and sometimes illicit signals between lovers. Looking over the countryside, Etzwane thought Frill an agreeable place, and he hoped that the balloon would land here, if for no other reason than to ease his aching body.

The wind-tender, for his part, had hoped to drift on into Canton Cathriy where the trade winds blowing in from Shellflower Bay would take him southwest to meet the Great Transverse Route somewhere in Canton Mai, but he had to reckon with his passengers. They had divided into two factions. The first had become impatient with hanging motionless in the still air and demanded that the balloon be put down; the second, to the contrary, feared that the wind would rise and sweep them to perdition out over the Green Ocean; they insisted even more emphatically that the balloon be lowered.

The wind-tender at last threw up his arms in vexation and valved out a quantity of gas until his altimeter indicated gradual descent. He opened his floor panel to inspect the terrain below and for the first time noticed Etzwane. He peered down in shock and suspicion, but he could be sure of nothing. And in any event he was powerless to act unless he chose to slide down one of the guy lines to confront the unauthorized passenger, which he did not care to do.

The guys sank into the thick blue grass of a meadow. Etzwane jumped gratefully out of the ring; the balloon, relieved of his weight, swung back aloft. Etzwane ran like a wild creature for the hedge. Heedless of cuts and scratches, he burst through the brambles and into a lane where he ran pell-mell until he came to a copse of yap-nut trees. He plunged into the shadows and stood till he caught his breath.

He could see nothing but foliage. Selecting the tallest tree in sight, he climbed until he could see over the hedge and across the meadow.

The balloon was down, anchored to a stump. The passengers had alighted and stood arguing with the wind-tender, demanding immediate fare rebates and expense money. This the wind-tender refused to pay over, in the certain knowledge that the main office clerks would not casually refund these sums unless he were able to produce detailed vouchers, invoices, and receipts.

The passengers began to grow ugly; the wind-tender at last resolved the matter by breaking loose the anchor and scrambling into the gondola. Relieved of the passengers, the balloon rose swiftly and drifted away, leaving the passengers in a disconsolate cluster.

For three weeks Etzwane roamed the country-side, a gaunt harsh-featured lad in the rags of his Pure Boy gown. In the heart of the yapnut grove he built a little den of twigs and leaves in which he maintained a tiny fire, blown up from a coal stolen at a farm house hearth. He stole other articles: an old jacket of green homespun, a lump of black sausage, a roll of coarse cord and a bundle of hay with which he planned to make himself a bed. The hay was insufficient; he returned for a second bundle and stole as well an old earthenware bowl with which the farmer fed his fowl. On this latter occasion, as he jumped from the back window of the barn, he was sighted by the boys of the farm, who gave chase and harried him through the woods until at last he went to cover in a dense thicket. He heard them destroying his den and exclaiming in anger at the stolen goods as they blundered past: "Yodel's ahulphs will winkle him out. They can take him back upland for their pains." Cold chills coursed down Etzwane's back. When the boys left the wood, he climbed the tall tree and watched them return to their farm. "They won't bring in ahulphs," he told himself in a hollow voice. "They'll forget all about me tomorrow. After all, it was just a bit of hay . . . An old coat . . ."

On the following day Etzwane kept an anxious watch on the farmhouse. When he saw the folk going about their normal duties, he became somewhat less fearful.

The next morning when he climbed the tree he

saw to his horror three ahulphs beside the barn. They were a lumpy dwarfish variety, with the look of hairy goblin-dogs: the Murtre Mountain strain. In a panic Etzwane leapt from the tree and set off through the woods toward the river Lurne. If luck were with him, he would find a boat or a raft; for he could not swim.

Leaving the forest, he crossed a field of purple moy; looking back, his worst fears were realized: the ahulphs came behind.

So far they had not sighted him; they ran with their eyes and foot-noses to the ground. With pounding legs and bumping heart, Etzwane ran from the field, up the highroad that paralleled the riverbank.

Along the road came a high-wheeled carriage drawn by a prime pacing bullock, the result of nine thousand years breeding. Though capable of a very smart pace, it moved in a leisurely fashion, as if the driver were in no great hurry to reach his destination. Etzwane pulled up the old jacket to hide his bare neck and called to the man who drove the carriage: "Please, sir, may I ride with you for a little bit?"

The man, reining the pacer to a halt, gave Etzwane a somber appraisal. Etzwane, returning the inspection, saw a lean man of indeterminate age with a pallid skin, a high forehead and austere nose, a shock of soft white hair neatly cropped, wearing a suit of fine gray cloth. The verticals of his torc were purple and gray; the horizontals were white and black, neither of which Etzwane could identify. He seemed very old, knowing and urbane, yet, on the other hand, not very old at all. He spoke in a voice of neutral courtesy: "Jump aboard. How far do you go?"

"I don't know," said Etzwane. "As far as possible. To be quite frank, the ahulphs are after me."

"Indeed? What is your crime?"

"Nothing of any consequence. The farmer boys consider me a vagabond and want to hunt me down."

"I can't very well assist fugitives," said the man, "but you may ride with me for a bit."

"Thank you."

The cart moved down the road, Etzwane keeping a watch behind. The man put a toneless question: "Where is your home?"

Etzwane could trust no one with this secret. "I have no home."

"And where is your destination?"

"Garwiy. I want to put a petition to the Faceless Man to help my mother."

"And how would he do this?"

Etzwane looked over his shoulder; the ahulphs were not yet in sight. "She is under unjust indenture and now must work in the tannery. The Faceless Man could order her indenture lifted; I'm sure she has paid it off and more, but they keep no reckonings."

"The Faceless Man is not likely to intervene in a matter of canton law."

"I've been told so. But perhaps he'll listen."

The man gave a faint smile. "The Faceless Man is gratified that canton law functions effectively. Can you believe that he'll disrupt old customs and turn everything topsy-turvy, even at Bashon?"

Etzwane looked at him in surprise. "How did you know?"

"Your gown. Your way of speech. Your mention of a tannery."

Etzwane had nothing to say. He looked over his shoulder, wishing the man would drive faster.

Even as he looked, the ahulphs bounded out into the road. Crouching down, Etzwane watched in sweating fascination. Through some peculiar working of their brain, a loss of scent confused them, and no amount of training or exhortation could persuade them to seek their quarry visually. Etzwane looked around at the man, who seemed more distant and austere than ever. The man said, "I won't be able to protect you. You must help yourself."

Etzwane turned back to watch the road. Over the hedge bounded the farmer's boys. The ahulphs made grinning disavowals, loping helpfully in one direction, then another. The boys gave a caw of rage at the helplessness of the ahulphs; then one saw the carriage and pointed. All began to run in hot pursuit.

Etzwane said anxiously, "Can't you drive somewhat faster? Otherwise they will kill me."

The man looked stonily ahead as if he had not heard. Etzwane gave a despairing glance behind, to find his pursuers gaining rapidly. His life was coming to an end. The ahulphs, with license to kill, would rend him apart at once, then carefully tie the parts into parcels to take home, quarreling over this and that as they did so. Etzwane jumped from the carriage, to tumble head over heels into the road. Scraped and bruised but feeling nothing, he sprang down the river bank, bursting through the alders and into the swift yellow Lurne. What now? He had never swam a stroke in his life. . . . He clutched to the twigs, shuddering uncontrollably, torn between dread of the water and a desire to immerse himself away from view. The ahulphs came crashing down the river bank, trying to push their hairy faces through the thicket. Etzwane eased himself downstream, clinging to the twigs, letting his legs float. The green jacket weighed on him; he slipped it off. Catching a bubble of air, it moved downstream, attracting the attention of the farm boys who could see only indistinctly through the brush. They ran shouting along the bank; Etzwane waited. Fifty yards downstream they discovered their mistake and stood arguing: Where was their quarry? They ordered one of the ahulphs to swim across the stream and range the opposite bank, to which the ahulph made whining protests. The boys drew back up the bank. Etzwane floated with the current, hoping to pass them unseen and presently pull himself to shore.

Silence on the bank: a sinister absence of sound. Etzwane's legs began to feel numb; cautiously he edged himself into the thicket. The disturbance attracted attention; one of the boys set up a halloo. Etzwane fell back into the water and, missing his grip on the twigs, was carried off into the stream. Straining to hold up his head, beating down with his arms, thrashing with his legs, Etzwane floundered out into midstream. His breath came in harsh gasps; water entered his mouth to choke him; he felt himself going down. The opposite bank was not too far away. He made a desperate final effort; one of his feet touched bottom. He pushed, thrust himself, hopping and lurching toward the bank. Kneeling in the shallows, clinging to the alders, he hung his head and gave himself up to hoarse racking coughs. From the far bank the boys jeered at him, and the ahulphs began to thrust down through the alders. Etzwane wearily tried to push through the brush, but the bank beyond loomed high and steep above him. He waded with the current. One of the ahulphs jumped into the stream and paddled directly toward Etzwane; the current carried him past. With all his force Etzwane threw a chunk of water-sodden timber. It struck the hairy dog-spider head; the creature keened and moaned and retreated to the opposite bank. Etzwane half-waded, half-hopped with the current, the boys and ahulphs keeping pace along the other bank. Suddenly they all ran forward pell-mell; looking down the stream, Etzwane saw a five-arched stone bridge and, beyond, the town. His pursuers intended to cross the bridge and come down the bank at him. Etzwane gauged the stream; he could never swim back across. He made a ferocious attack on the alders, ignoring scratches, jabs, cuts; at length he pulled himself to the bank, a vertical rise of six feet overgrown with fern and thorn-grass. He scrambled halfway up, to fall moaning back into the alders. Once again he tried, clinging with fingernails, elbows, chin, knees. By the most precarious of margins he crawled up and over, to lie flat on his face at the edge of the riverside lane. He could not rest an instant. Glassy-eyed, he heaved himself first to his hands and knees, then to his feet.

Only fifty yards away the town began. Across

the lane, in a wooded park, he saw a half-dozen carts painted in gay symbols of pale pink, white, purple, pale green, blue.

Etzwane staggered forward, flapping his arms; he ran up to a short sour-faced man of middle-age who sat on a stool sipping hot broth from a cup.

Etzwane composed himself as best he could, but his voice was tremulous and hoarse. "I am Gastel Etzwane; take me into your troupe. Look; I wear no torc. I am a musician."

The short man drew back in surprise and irritation. "Get along with you; do you think we clasp every passing rascal to our bosoms? We are adepts; this is our standard of excellence; go dance a jig in the market square."

Down the road came the ahulphs and behind the farm boys.

Etzwane cried, "I am no rascal; my father was Dystar the druithine; I play the khitan." He searched wildly about; he saw a nearby instrument and seized it. His fingers were weak and water-soaked; he tried to play a run of chords and produced only a jangle.

A black-furred hand seized his shoulder and pulled; another took his arm and jerked another direction; the ahulphs fell to disputing which had touched him first.

The musician rose to his feet. He seized a length of firewood and struck furiously at both ahulphs. "Goblins, be off; do you dare touch a musician?"

The peasant youths came forward. "Musician? He is a common thief, a vagabond. We intend to kill him and protect our hard-earned goods."

The musician threw down a handful of coins.

"A musician takes what he needs; he never steals.
Pick up your money and go."

The farm boys made surly sounds and glared
at Etzwane. Grudgingly they picked the coins out
of the dirt and departed, the ahulphs yelping and
dancing sideways. Their work was for naught;
they would receive neither money nor meat.

The musician once more settled upon his
stool. "Dystar's son, you say. What a sorry let-
down. Well, it can't be helped. Throw away those
rags; have the women give you a jacket and a
meal. Then come let me see what is to be done."

Chapter 6

Clean, warm, full of bread and soup, Etzwane came cautiously back to Frolitz, who sat at a table under the trees, a flagon of liquor at his elbow. Etzwane sat down on a bench and watched. Frolitz fitted a new reed to the mouthpiece of a wood-horn. Etzwane waited. Frolitz apparently intended to ignore his presence.

Etzwane hitched himself forward. "Do you intend to let me stay with the troupe, sir?"

Frolitz turned his head. "We are musicians, boy. We demand a great deal from each other."

"I would do my best," said Etzwane.

"It might not be good enough. String up that instrument yonder."

Etzwane took up the khitan and did as he was bid. Frolitz grunted. "Now tell me how Dystar's son runs the fields in rags?"

"I was born at Bashon in Canton Bastern," said Etzwane. "A musician named Feld Maijesto gave me a khitan, which I learned to play as best as I could. I did not care to become a Chilite, and I ran away."

"That is a lucid exposition," said Frolitz. "I am acquainted with Feld, who takes a rather casual attitude toward his craft. I make serious demands upon my folk; we are not slackers here. What if I send you away?"

"I will go to Garwiy and ask the Faceless Man

to give me a musician's torc and to help my mother as well."

Frolitz looked up at the sky. "What illusions the young harbor nowadays! So now the Faceless Man indulges every ragamuffin who comes to Garwiy with a grievance!"

"He must heed grievances; how else can he rule? Surely he wants the folk of Shant to be content!"

"Hard to say what the Faceless Man wants. But it's not good policy talking. He might be listening from behind that wagon, and he's said to be thin-skinned. Look yonder on the tree. Only last night, while I slept fifty feet away, that placard was posted! It gives an eerie feeling."

Etzwane examined the placard. It read:

The ANOME is Shant!
Shant is the ANOME!
Which is to say: The ANOME is everywhere!
Sly sarcasm is folly.
Disrespect is sedition.
With benevolent attention! With fervent zeal!
With puissant determination!
The ANOME works for Shant!

Etzwane nodded soberly. "This is exactly correct. Who posted the placard?"

"How should I know?" snapped Frolitz. "Perhaps the Faceless Man himself. If I were he, I'd enjoy going about making guilty folk jump. Still it's not wise to attract his notice with petitions and demands. If they are right and reasonable— so much the worse."

"What do you mean?"

"Use your head, lad! Suppose you and the canton have come into conflict, and you want matters altered. You go into Garwiy and present a petition which is right and proper and just. The Faceless Man has three choices. He can accommodate you and put the canton into an uproar, with unknown consequences. He can deny your just petition and expect sedition every time you get drunk in a tavern and start to talk. Or he can quietly take your head."

Etzwane pondered. "You mean that I shouldn't take my grievance to the Faceless Man?"

"He's the last man to take a grievance to!"

"Then what should I do?"

"Just what you're doing. Become a musician and make a living complaining of your woe. But remember: Complain of your own woe! Don't complain of the Faceless Man! . . . What's that you're playing now?"

Etzwane, having strung the khitan, had touched forth a few chords. He said, "Nothing in particular. I don't know too many tunes. Only what I learned from the musicians who came along the road."

"Halt, halt, halt!" cried Frolitz, covering his ears. "What are these strange noises, these original discords?"

Etzwane licked his lips. "Sir, it is a melody of my own contriving."

"But this is impertinence! You consider the standard works beneath your dignity? What of the repertory I have labored to acquire? You tell me now that I have wasted my time, that henceforth I must attend only the outpourings of your natural genius?"

Etzwane at last was able to insert a disclaimer.

"No, no, sir, by no means! I have never been able to hear the famous works; I was forced to play tunes I thought up myself."

"Well, so long as it doesn't become an obsession—Not so much thumb there. What of the rattle-box? Do you think it's there for show?"

"No sir. I hurt my elbow somewhat today."

"Well, then, why scratch aimlessly at the khitan? Let's hear a tune on the wood-horn."

Etzwane looked dubiously at the instrument, which was tied together with string. "I've never had the sleight of it."

"What?" Frolitz gaped in disbelieving shock. "Well, then, learn it! The tringolet, the clarion, the tipple as well. We are musicians in this troupe, not, like Feld and his scamping cronies, a set of theorizing dilettantes. Here, take this wood-horn; go play scales. After a bit I'll come by and listen."

A year later Master Frolitz brought his troupe to Garwiy, Etzwane now wearing a musician's torc. This was a locality the wandering troupes visited but seldom, for the urbane folk of Garwiy enjoyed novelty, style, and topical substance in preference to music. Etzwane, paying no heed to Frolitz's advice, went to the Corporation Plaza and stood in line at the booth where petitions to the Faceless Man might be filed for five florins. A placard reassured those who waited:

All petitions are seen by the ANOME!

The same scrupulous judgment is applied to the problems of all, if their petition costs five or five hundred florins. Be concise and

definite, state the exact deficiency or hardship, specify the precise solution you propose. Merely because you are filing a petition does not indicate that your cause is
just; conceivably you are wrong and your
adversary right. Be instructed, rather than
disappointed, should the ANOME yield a
negative response.

The ANOME administers equity, not bounty!

Etzwane paid his five florins, received a form
from the desk. In the most careful language he
stated his case, citing the cynicism of the Chilites
in respect to the indentures of the women. "In
particular, the lady Eathre has more than paid
her obligation to the Ecclesiarch Osso Higajou,
but he has assigned her to work in the tannery.
I pray that you order this injustice terminated,
that the lady Eathre may be free to select the
future course of her life without reference to the
wishes of Ecclesiarch Osso."

Occasionally the five-florin petitions encountered slow responses; Etzwane's, however, received
a verdict on the following day. All petitions and
their responses were deemed in the public interest and posted openly on a board; with trembling fingers Etzwane pulled down the response
coded with his torc colors.

The response read:

The ANOME notes with sympathy a son's
concern for the welfare of his mother. The
laws of Canton Bastern are definite. They
require that before an indenture can be
considered paid, the indentured person must

display a receipt and balance sheet for all monies paid over by the person and all charges incurred and debited against the same person's account. Sometimes a person consumes food, lodging, clothing, education, entertainment, medicine, and the like, in excess of his or her earnings, whereupon the payment of an indenture may be delayed. Such is possibly true in the present case.

The judgment is this: I command the Ecclesiarch Osso Higajou, upon presentation of this document, to render free the person of the lady Eathre, provided that she can show a favorable balance of one thousand five hundred florins, or if some person pays in cash to Ecclesiarch Osso Higajou one thousand five hundred florins, when it will be assumed that a previous balance between credit and debit exists.

In short, take this document and one thousand five hundred florins to Ecclesiarch Osso; he must deliver to you your mother, the lady Eathre.

With hope and encouragement,
THE ANOME

Etzwane became furiously angry. He instantly purchased a second petition and wrote: "Where can I get one thousand five hundred florins? I earn a hundred florins a year. Eathre has paid Osso twice over; will you lend me one thousand five hundred florins?"

As before, the response was prompt. It read:

The ANOME regrets that he cannot lend either private or public funds for the settlement of indentures. The previous judgment remains the definitive verdict.

Etzwane wandered back to Fontenay's Inn where Frolitz made his Garwiy headquarters and wondered how or where he could lay his hands on one thousand five hundred florins.

Five years later, at Maschein in Canton Maseach, on the south slope of the Hwan, Etzwane encountered his father Dystar. The troupe, coming into town late, was at liberty for the evening. Etzwane and Fordyce, a youth three or four years older—Etzwane was now about eighteen—wandered through town, from one tavern to the next, gathering gossip and listening with critical ears to what music was being played.

At the Double Fish Inn they heard Master Rickard Oxtot's Gray-Blue-Green Interpolators.* During an intermission Etzwane fell into a discussion with the khitan-player, who minimized his own abilities. "To hear the khitan played in proper fashion, step across the way to the Old Caraz and hear the druithine."

Fordyce and Etzwane presently crossed to the Old Caraz and took goblets of effervescent green punch. The druithine sat in a corner gazing

---

* The language of Shant allows exquisite discrimination between colors. Against *red, scarlet, carmine, maroon, pink, vermilion, cerise,* Shant could set sixty descriptive degrees, with as many for every other color. In *Gray-Blue-Green* Interpolators, the qualities of "gray," "blue," and "green" were precisely specified in order to express by symbological means the exact emotional point of view from which Master Oxtot's troupe performed their variations.

moodily at the audience: a tall man with black-
gray hair, a strong nervous body, the face of a
dreamer dissatisfied with his dreams. He touched
his khitan, tuned one of the strings, struck a few
chords, listened as if displeased. His dark gaze
wandered the room, rested on Etzwane, passed
on. Again he began to play: slowly, laboriously
working around the edges of a melody, reaching
here, searching there, testing this, trying that,
like an absent-minded man raking leaves in a
wind. Insensibly the music became easier, more
certain; the lank themes, the incommensurate
rhythms, fused into an organism with a soul:
every note played had been preordained and necessary.

Etzwane listened in wonder. The music was
remarkable, played with majestic conviction and
a total absence of effort. Almost casually, the
druithine imparted heartbreaking news; he told
of golden oceans and unattainable islands; he
reported the sweet futility of life, then, with a
wry double beat and an elbow at the scratch-box,
supplied solutions to all the apparent mysteries.

His meal, hot pickled land crab with barley,
melon balls dusted with pollen, had been splendid but not copious; payment* had long been

* Druithines, unlike the troupes, never advertised their
comings and goings; after an unheralded, almost furtive
arrival at some locality, the druithine would visit one of
the taverns and order a repast, sumptuous or frugal, according to his whim or personal flair. Then, he would
bring forth his khitan and play but would not eat until
someone in the audience had paid for his meal. The
"uneaten meal," indeed, was a common jocular reference.
Druithines in decline reputedly employed a person to
make ostentatious payment for the meal as soon as it was

made. He had taken a flask of Gurgel's Elixir; another stood at his elbow, but he seemed uninterested in further drink. The music dwindled and departed into silence, like a caravan passing over the horizon.

Fordyce leaned over, put a question to one who sat nearby: "What is the druithine's name?"

"That is Dystar."

Fordyce turned marveling to Etzwane. "It is your father!"

Etzwane, with no words to say, gave a curt nod.

Fordyce rose to his feet. "Let me tell him that his natural son is here, who plays the khitan in his own right."

"No," said Etzwane. "Please don't speak to him."

Fordyce sat down slowly. "Why not, then?"

Etzwane heaved a deep sigh. "Perhaps he has many natural sons. A good number may play the khitan. He might not care to give polite attention to each of these."

Fordyce shrugged and said no more.

Once more Dystar struck at his khitan, to play music that told of a man striding through the night, halting from time to time to muse upon one or another of the stars.

For a reason Etzwane could not define, he became uncomfortable. Between himself and this man whom he did not know existed a tension. He had no claim against him; he could reproach him

---

set forth. After the meal the druithine's further income depended on gratuities, gifts from the tavern-keeper, engagements at private parties or in the manor houses of aristocrats. A druithine of talent might become wealthy, as he had few expenses.

for no fault of omission or commission; his debt to Eathre had been precisely that of all the other men who had stepped into her cottage from Rhododendron Way; like the others he had paid in full and gone his way. Etzwane made no attempt to fathom the workings of his mind. He made an excuse to Fordyce and departed the Old Caraz. In a deep depression he wandered back to camp, Eathre's image before his mind. He cursed himself for negligence, for lack of diligence. He had saved little money—though for a fact he earned little enough. This was as it should be; Etzwane had no complaint. In addition to sustenance Frolitz provided instruction and opportunity to play. Musicians other than druithines seldom became wealthy, a situation that persuaded many troupers to try their luck as druithines. A few succeeded; most, finding the cost of their meals undischarged, attempted to enliven their performances with bravura effects, eccentric mannerisms, or when all else failed, singing songs with khitan accompaniment to audiences of peasants, children, and the musically illiterate.

Back at the camp Etzwane turned dark thoughts back and forth in his mind. He had no illusions; at his present competence, with his present experience of life, he was incapable of becoming a druithine. What of the future? His life with Master Frolitz was satisfactory enough; did he want more? He went to his locker and brought forth his khitan; sitting on the steps of the cart, he began to play the slow music, pensive and melancholy, to which the folk of Canton Ifwiy liked to step their pavannes. The music sounded dry, contrived, lifeless. Remembering the supple, urgent music that surged from Dystar's khitan as if it had its own life, Etzwane became first grim, then sad, then bitterly angry—at Dystar, at himself. He put up the khitan and laid himself into his bunk where he tried to order his whirling young mind.

Another five years passed. Master Frolitz and the Pink-Black-Azure-Deep Greeners, as he now called his troupe, came to Brassei in Canton Elphine, not a great distance from Garwiy. Etzwane had grown into a slight, nervously muscular young man, with a face somber and austere. His hair was black, his skin darkly sallow; his mouth hung in a slightly crooked droop; he was neither voluble, gay, nor gregarious; his voice was soft and spare, and only when he had taken wine did he seem to become easy or spontaneous. Certain of the musicians thought him supercilious, others thought him vain; only Master Frolitz sought out his company, to the puzzlement of all, for Frolitz was warm where Etzwane was cold, forward where Etzwane stepped aside. When taxed with his partiality, Frolitz only scoffed; for a fact he found Etzwane a good listener, a wry and taciturn foil to his own volubility.

After establishing camp on Brassei Common, Frolitz, with Etzwane for company, made the rounds of the city's taverns and music halls, to learn the news and solicit work. During the late evening they came to Zerkow's Inn, a cavernous structure of old timber and whitewashed marl. Posts supported a roof of a dozen crazy angles; from the beams hung mementos of all the years of the inn's existence: grotesque wooden faces blackened by grime and smoke, dusty glass animals, the skull of an ahulph, three dried cauls, an iron meteorite, a collection of heraldic balls, much more. At the moment Zerkow's was almost deserted, due to the weekly rigor ordained by Paraplastus, the local Cosmic Lord of Creation. Frolitz approached Loy the innkeeper and made his proposals. While the two chaffered, Etzwane stood to the side, absent-mindedly studying the placards on the posts. Preoccupied with his own concerns, he observed nothing of what he read. This morning he had received a large sum of money, an unexpected sum that had substantially augmented his savings. Sufficiently? For the twentieth time he cast up a reckoning; for the twentieth time he arrived at the same figure, on the borderline between adequacy and inadequacy. Yet where would he get more? Certainly not from Frolitz, not for a month or more. But time passed; with his goal so near he itched with impatience. His eyes focused on the placards, for the most part standard exhortations to probity:

The BLANK, being faceless, shows the same semblance to all. Whom no man knows, no man can suborn.

Obey all edicts with alacrity! The casual bystander may be the UNKNOWN FORCE himself!

Lucky folk of Shant! In sixty-two cantons sing praise! How can evil flourish when every act is subject to the scrutiny of the GLORIOUS ANOME?

The posters were printed in magenta, signifying grandeur, on a field of grayed pink, the color of omnipotence.

On the wall hung a bulletin, somewhat larger,

printed in the brown and black of emergency:

> Warning! Take care! Several large bands of Roguskhoi have recently been observed along the slopes of the Hwan! These noxious creatures may not be approached, at sure peril of your life!

Frolitz and Loy came to mutually satisfactory terms: on the following night Frolitz would bring in the Pink-Black-Azure-Deep Greeners for a two- or three-week engagement. In recognition of the understanding Loy served Etzwane a free tankard of green cider. Etzwane asked, "When was the black-brown put up?"

"About the Roguskhoi? Two or three days ago. They made a raid down into Canton Shallou and kidnaped a dozen women."

"The Faceless Man should act," said Etzwane. "The least he can do is protect us; isn't that his function? Why do we wear these torcs otherwise?"

Frolitz, conversing with a stranger in traveler's clothes who had just entered the tavern, took time to speak over his shoulder: "Pay no heed to the lad; he has no knowledge of the world."

Loy, puffing out his fat cheeks, ignored Frolitz instead. "It's no secret that something must be done. I've heard ugly reports of the creatures. It seems that they're swarming like ants up in the Hwan. There aren't females, you know, just males."

"How do they breed?" Etzwane wondered. "It is a matter I can't understand."

"They use ordinary women, with great enthusiasm, or so I'm told, and the issue is always male."

"Peculiar . . . Where would such creatures come from?"

"Palasedra," declared Loy wisely. "You must know the direction of Palasedran science: always breeding, always forcing, never satisfied with creatures the way they are. I say, and others agree, that an unruly strain slipped out of the Palasedran forcing houses and crossed the Great Salt Bog into Shant. To our great misfortune."

"Unless they come to spend their florins at Zerkow's!" Frolitz called down the bar. "Since they're great drinkers, that's the way to handle them: keep them in drink and in debt."

Loy shook his head dubiously. "They'd drive away my other trade. Who wants to bump beakers with a murderous red-faced demon two feet taller than himself? I say, order them back to Palasedra without delay."

"That may be the best way," said Frolitz, "but is it the practical way? Who will issue the order?"

"There's an answer to that," said Etzwane. "The Faceless Man must exert himself. Is he not omnipotent? Is he not ubiquitous?" He jerked his thumb toward the pink and magenta placards. "Such are his claims."

Frolitz spoke in a hoarse whisper to the stranger. "Etzwane wants the Faceless Man to go up into the Hwan and torc all the Roguskhoi."

"As good a way as any," said Etzwane with a sour grin.

Into the tavern burst a young man, a porter employed at Zerkow's. "Have you heard? At Makkaby's Warehouse, not half an hour ago, a burglar got his head taken. The Faceless Man is nearby!"

Everyone in the room looked around. "Are you

certain?" demanded Loy. "There might have been a swash-trap set out."

"No, without question: the torc took his head. The Faceless Man caught him in the act."

"Fancy that!" Loy marveled. "The warehouse is only a step down the street!"

Frolitz turned to lean back against the bar. "There you have it," he told Etzwane. "You complain: 'Why does not the Faceless Man act?' Almost while you speak he acts. Is not that your answer?"

"Not entirely."

Frolitz swallowed half a tankard of the strong green cider and winked at the stranger: a tall, thin man with a head of soft white hair, an expression of austere acquiescence toward the vicissitudes of life. His age was indeterminate; he might have been old or young. "The burglar suffered a harsh fate," Frolitz told Etzwane. "The lesson to be learned is this: Never commit an unlawful act. Especially, never steal; when you take a man's property, your life becomes forfeit, as has just been demonstrated."

Loy rubbed his chin with uneasy fingers. "In a sense, the penalty seems extreme. The burglar took goods but lost his life. These are the laws of Elphine which the Faceless Man correctly enforced—but should a bagful of goods and a man's life weigh so evenly on the balance?"

The white-haired stranger offered his opinion. "Why should it be otherwise? You ignore a crucial factor in the situation. Property and life are not incommensurable, when property is measured in terms of human toil. Essentially property is life; it is that proportion of life which an individual has expended to gain the property. When a thief steals property, he steals life. Each act of pillage therefore becomes a small murder."

Frolitz struck the bar with his fist. "A sound exposition, if ever I heard one! Loy, place before this instructive stranger a draft of his own choice, at my expense. Sir, how may I address you?"

The stranger told Loy: "A mug of that green cider, if you please." He turned somewhat upon his chair, toward Frolitz and Etzwane. "My name is Ifness; I am a traveling mercantilist."

Etzwane gave him a sour look; his rancor toward the man in the pacer trap had never waned. Ifness, then, was his name. A mercantilist? Etzwane had his doubts. Not so Frolitz. "Odd to hear such clever theories from a mercantilist!" he marveled.

"The talk of such folk is often humdrum," agreed Loy. "For sheer entertainment, give me the company of a tavern-keeper."

Ifness pursed his lips judiciously. "All folk, mercantilists as well as tavern-keepers and musicians, try to relate their work to abstract universals. We mercantilists are highly sensitive to theft, which stabs at our very essence. To steal is to acquire goods by a simple, informal, and inexpensive process. To buy identical goods is tedious, irksome, and costly. Is it any wonder that larceny is popular? Nonetheless it voids the mercantilist's reasons for being alive; we regard thieves with the same abhorrence that musicians might feel for a fanatic gang which beat bells and gongs whenever musicians played."

Frolitz stifled an ejaculation.

Ifness tasted the mug of green cider that Loy had set before him. "To repeat: when a thief steals property, he steals life. For a mercantilist

I am tolerant of human weakness, and I would not react vigorously to the theft of a day. I would resent the theft of a week; I would kill the thief who stole a year of my life."

"Hear, hear!" cried Frolitz. "Words to deter the criminal! Etzwane, have you listened?"

"You need not single me out so pointedly," said Etzwane. "I am no thief."

Frolitz, somewhat elevated by his drafts of cider, told Ifness, "Quite true, quite true! He is not a thief, he is a musician! Owing to the virtue of my instruction, he has become an adept! He finds time for nothing but study. He is master of six instruments; he knows the parts to two thousand compositions. When I forget a chord, he is always able to call out a signal. This morning, mark you, I paid over to him a bonus of three hundred florins, out of the troupe's instrument fund."

Ifness nodded approvingly. "He seems a paragon."

"To a certain extent," said Frolitz. "On the other hand, he is secretive and stubborn. He nurtures and nurses every florin he has ever seen; he would breed them together if he could. All this makes him a dull dog at a debauch. As for the three hundred florins, I long ago had promised him five hundred and decided to stint him for his cheerlessness."

"But will not this method augment his gloom?"

"To the contrary; I keep him keen. As a musician he must learn to be grateful for every trifle. I have made him what he is, at least in his better parts. For his faults you must cite a certain Chilite, Osso, whom Etzwane claims as his 'soul-father.'"

"On my way east I will be passing through Canton Bastern," said Ifness politely. "If I encounter Osso, I will convey him your greetings."

"Don't bother," said Etzwane. "I am going to Bashon myself."

Frolitz jerked around to focus his eyes on Etzwane. "Did I hear correctly? You mentioned no such plans to me!"

"If I had, you would not have paid me three hundred florins this morning. As a matter of fact I just made up my mind ten seconds ago."

"But what of the troupe? What of our engagements? Everything will be discommoded!"

"I won't be gone long. When I return, you can pay me more money since I seem to be indispensable."

Frolitz raised his bushy eyebrows. "No one is indispensable save myself! I'll play khitan and wood-horn together, if I feel so inclined, and produce better music than any four fat-necked apprentices!" Frolitz banged his mug on the bar by way of emphasis. "However, to keep my friend Loy satisfied, I must hire a substitute—an added expense and worry. How long will you be gone?"

"Three weeks, I suppose."

" 'Three weeks'?" roared Frolitz. "Are you planning a rest cure on the Ilwiy beach? Three days to Bashon, twenty minutes for your business, three days back to Brassei: that's enough!"

"Well enough, if I traveled by balloon," said Etzwane. "I must walk or ride a wagon."

"Is this more parsimony? Why not go by balloon? What is the difference in cost?"

"Something like thirty florins each way, or so I would guess."

"Well, then! Where is your pride? Does a Pink-

Black-Azure-Deep Greener travel like a dog-barber?" He turned to Loy the publican. "Give this man sixty florins, in advance, on my account."

Somewhat dubiously Loy went to his till. Frolitz took the money and clapped it down on the bar in front of Etzwane. "There you are; be off with you. Above all, do not let yourself be deceived by other troupe-masters. They might offer more money than I pay, but be assured, there would be hidden disadvantages!"

Etzwane laughed. "Never fear, I'll be back perhaps in a week or ten days. I'll take the first balloon out; my business at Bashon will be short enough; then it's the first balloon back to Brassei."

Frolitz turned to consult Ifness but found an empty chair; Ifness had departed the tavern.

Chapter 7

A storm had struck in from the Green Ocean, bringing floods to Cantons Maiy and Erevan; a section of the Great Transverse Route had been washed out; balloons were delayed two days until crews were able to rig an emergency pass-over.

Etzwane was able to secure a place on the first balloon out of Brassei, the *Asper*. He climbed into the gondola and took a seat; behind him came other passengers. Last aboard was Ifness.

Etzwane sat indifferently, making no sign of recognition. Ifness saw Etzwane and after the briefest of hesitations nodded and sat down beside him. "It seems that we are to be traveling companions."

Etzwane made a cool response. "I will find it a pleasure."

The door was closed; bars were lowered to provide the passengers a grip when the balloon swayed and heeled. The wind-tender entered his compartment, tested the winches, checked valves and ballast release. He signaled the ground crew; they rolled the Judas-dolly out along the slot; the *Asper* rose into the air. The running dolly was released; the *Asper* danced and flounced in the beam wind until the wind-tender trimmed guys, whereupon the *Asper* steadied and surged ahead, with taut guys and singing dolly.

Ifness spoke to Etzwane: "You seem totally relaxed. Have you ridden the balloon-way before?"

"Many years ago."

"A wonderful experience for a child."

"It was indeed."

"I am never altogether comfortable in the balloons," said Ifness. "They seem so frail and vulnerable. A few sticks, the thinnest of membranes, the most fugitive of gases. Still, the Palasedran gliders seem even more precarious: transport, no doubt, which accords with their temperament. You are bound for Bashon, I understand."

"I intend to pay off my mother's indenture."

Ifness reflected a moment. "Perhaps you should have entrusted your business to a job-broker. The Chilites are a devious folk and may try to mulct you."

"No doubt they'll try. But it won't do any good. I carry an ordinance from the Faceless Man, which they must obey."

"I see. Well, I still would be on my guard. The Chilites, for all their unworldliness, are seldom bested."

After a moment Etzwane said, "You seem well acquainted with the Chilites."

Ifness permitted himself a faint smile. "They are a fascinating cult; the Chilite rationale and its physical projection make a most elegant pattern. You don't follow me? Consider: a group which nightly intoxicates itself into a frenzy of erotic hallucinations under the pretext of religious asceticism—isn't this sublime insouciance? A social machinery is necessary to maintain this state of affairs: it is as you know. How to ensure persistence in a group not itself regenerative? By recruiting the children of other men, by the constant infusion of new blood. How to secure so

precious a commodity, which other men normally protect with their lives? By the ingenious in-
stitution of Rhododendron Way, which also turns
a good profit. What marvelous effrontery! It can
almost be admired!"

Etzwane was surprised to find Ifness so en-
thusiastic. He said coldly, "I was born on Rhododendron Way and became a Pure Boy; I find
them disgusting."

Ifness seemed amused. He said, "They are a
remarkable adaptation, if perhaps too highly spe-
cialized. What would happen, for instance, if
they no longer could obtain galga? In a genera-
tion or less the structure of the society would
alter in one of several conceivable directions."

Etzwane wondered that a mercantilist should
be so apt at abstract analysis of human society.
"What sort of goods do you sell?" he asked. "As a
mercantilist I assume that you sell goods."

"Not quite the case," said Ifness. "I am employed by a mercantile association to travel here
and there and discover possible new applications
for their products."

"It seems an interesting job," said Etzwane.

"I find it so."

Etzwane glanced at the man's torc. "From the
purple-green I assume your home to be Garwiy."

"That is the case." Ifness took a journal from
his valise, *The Kingdoms of Old Caraz*, and began
to read.

Etzwane looked out over the reaches of the
landscape. An hour passed. The *Asper* halted at
a siding to allow a pair of eastbound balloons
to skim by, cables taut, dollies singing down the
slots.

At noon the wind-tender sold tea, slabs of fruit jelly, buns, and meat sticks to those who required food. Ifness put away his journal and ate; Etzwane preferred to husband his funds, which were barely sufficient. Finishing his meal, Ifness fastidiously brushed his hands and returned to the journal.

An hour later the *Asper* arrived at Brassei Junction in Canton Fairlea and was switched onto the Great Transverse Route. The wind freshened but, coming from the port quarter, blew the balloon only at its own speed; so passed the afternoon. At sunset the wind died completely, and the *Asper* stood becalmed above an upland moor, in Canton Shade.

The suns danced down behind the horizon; the sky flared violet behind four streaks of apple-green cloud. Darkness came quickly. A breeze stirred the upper air, still coming from astern; the *Asper* eased forward along the slot, no faster than a man could walk.

The wind-tender served a meal of cheese, wine, and biscuits, then rigged hammocks. The passengers, with nothing better to do, slept.

Late the next afternoon the *Asper* arrived at Angwin, at the head of the great Gorge. Here the slot terminated, and the cable swung up in a pair of great pale swags to Angwin Junction where years before—it seemed dream-time—Etzwane had been brought up from Carbade to work as an apprentice. He wondered if Finnerack still worked there.

The *Asper* was scheduled to continue along the Great Transverse Route, to the south slopes of the Hwan; at Angwin it descended to discharge

those passengers who were to continue along the
North Spur. There were four of these: Etzwane,
a pair of commercial buyers bound for Dublay at
the tip of Canton Cape, and Ifness.

The North Spur connection, which should
have been waiting, had been delayed by light
winds; the four passengers must put up a night
at Angwin Inn.

The *Asper* climbed back into the sky, with the
guys now shifted to the cable. In the wheelhouse
under the inn the crew put their shoulders to the
windlass; the balloon was drawn across the Great
Gorge and up to Junction. Etzwane could not
bring himself to go down to watch the windlass,
as did the two buyers.

Later Etzwane and the buyers sat in the
lounge overlooking the Great Gorge; Ifness had
gone for a stroll along the rim of the chasm.

The suns toppled low, one behind the other;
magenta light struck Mount Mish and the far
peaks beyond. The gorge became dim with murk.
Etzwane and the buyers drank spiced cider; as
the steward brought a tray of preserved fruit, one
of the buyers asked, "Do you see many Roguskhoi
down in the gorge?"

"Not often," the steward replied. "The lads up
at Junction used to see a few, but from what I
hear, they've migrated east into the Wildlands."

"They raided down in Shallou not so long
ago," said the second buyer. "That's to the west."

"Yes, so it is. Well, it's all beyond me. What
we'd do if a band attacked Angwin, I can't imagine."

The other buyer spoke. "The gorge itself is
some protection, so I should think."

The steward looked gloomily down into the blue murk. "Not enough to suit me if what I hear of the devils is true. If we had women up here, I wouldn't sleep nights. They hardly go out of their way to kill a man except for entertainment, but if they smell a woman, they climb through fire and flood. In my opinion something ought to be done."

Ifness, who had returned unobserved, spoke from the shadows. "What, in your opinion, is the 'something' that ought to be done?"

"The Faceless Man should be notified and have it driven home to him, that's what! I say, throw a cordon around the whole Hwan if it takes every man in Shant and then start closing in, driving the devils together, killing as we go. When men from the north, east, south, and west look at each other over the top of Mount Skarack, then we'll know we're rid of the vermin."

One of the buyers demurred. "Too complicated; it would never work. They'd hide in caves or tunnels. Now, my idea is to put out poison—"

The other buyer offered a lewd specification for efficacious bait.

"Well, why not," demanded his colleague, "if it'll draw them? But poison's the answer, mark my words."

The second buyer said, "Don't be too sure! These are not animals, you know. They're freak men from across the Salt Bog. The Palasedrans have been quiet too long; it's unnatural, and now they're sending in the Roguskhoi."

The steward said, "I don't care where they come from; let's clear them out, back to Palasedra for preference. According to the afternoon news, just in over the radio, a band came down from Mount Haghead to raid a village in Morningshore. Killed, raped, kidnaped. The village is a total ruin."

"So far to the east?" murmured Ifness.

"That's the report. First Shallou to the west, then Morningshore to the east. The Hwan must be crawling with them."

"That doesn't necessarily follow," said Etzwane.

"You may be sure," said the first buyer in a pontifical voice, "that the Faceless Man is ready to act. He has no choice."

The steward sneered. "He's far away in Garwiy; what's our safety to him?"

The buyers pursed their lips. "Well," said one, "I wouldn't go so far as that. The Faceless Man represents us all! By and large he does a good job."

"Still," said the other, "the time has come. He should take action."

The steward inquired, "Do you gentlemen require more drink before supper? If so, call out now before cook strikes the gong."

Etzwane asked, "Is Dagbolt still superintendent?"

"No, old Dagbolt's been dead five years of throat chancre," replied the steward. "I knew him a mere three months, more than ample. Dickon Defonso is superintendent, and affairs go tolerably well."

"Does a certain Finnerack work at Angwin?"

"Finnerack? Somewhere I've heard the name. But he's not here."

"Might he be at Junction?"

"Nor at Junction. Finnerack . . . Some sort of scandal. Was he the criminal who loosed a balloon?"

"I couldn't say."

In the middle of the morning the balloon *Jano* arrived at Angwin. The four passengers climbed aboard; the *Jano* rose to the extent of its guys and was pulled back across the gorge to Junction. Etzwane gazed down in fascination at the little island in the sky. There the three great sheaves, almost in contact; there the stone shelter with the timber door and the outhouse cantilevered over the gorge. At the sheave he saw the motion of the man on duty; the balloon gave a jerk as the claw-jack drew down the guys and the grip was transferred to the North Spur cable, and another jerk as the jerk was released. Etzwane smiled as he thought of another balloon, so long ago. . . .

The *Jano* was drawn down to the North Station; the guys were transferred to a dolly; then off down the slot into Canton Seamus ran the *Jano,* tacking into a brisk breeze off the starboard bow. With the balloon trimmed to best advantage, the wind-tender came into the gondola. "All here for Oswiy, I take it?"

"Not I," said Etzwane. "I'm for Bastern Station at Carbade."

"Bastern Station? I'll put you down if the landing crew is on hand. They took themselves into Carbade during the raid."

"What raid is this?"

"You wouldn't have heard. The Roguskhoi, a band of fifty or sixty, pushed out of the wildlands and plundered down the Mirk."

"How far down the Mirk?"

"That I don't know. If they turned toward Seamus, you won't find a crew at Bastern Station. Why not go on down to Ascalon? You'd find it more secure."

"I must get off at Bastern Station if I slide down the guys."

When the *Jano* reached Bastern Station, the crew had returned to duty; the *Jano* was hauled down with a nervous jerkiness. Etzwane jumped to the ground; Ifness followed. "I take it that you are traveling east?" asked Ifness.

"Yes, to Bashon."

"I propose, then, that we share a vehicle."

Etzwane calculated his probable expense. Fifteen hundred florins for the indenture, a hundred for the return to Brassei with Eathre, another fifty for unforeseen contingencies. Sixteen hundred and fifty. He carried sixteen hundred and sixty-five. "I can't afford anything expensive," he said in a somewhat surly voice. Of all the folk of Shant, he least of all wished to be under obligation to Ifness. Save perhaps his soul-father Osso.

At the hostelry Ifness ordered a fast trap drawn by a pair of prime pacers. "I'll have to take two hundred florins from you," the hostler told Ifness. "That is the deposit. Hire will be twenty florins a day."

Etzwane said flatly, "I can't afford it." Ifness made an indifferent gesture. "It is how I choose to travel. Pay what you can; I will be satisfied."

"It's not much," said Etzwane. "Fifteen florins, in fact. Were it not for the Roguskhoi, I'd walk."

"Pay fifteen florins or nothing whatever," said Ifness. "It's all the same to me."

Nettled by the condescension, the more irritating for its absent-minded quality, Etzwane brought forth fifteen florins. "If this satisfies you, take it. Otherwise I will walk."

"Well enough, well enough; let us be off; I am anxious to inspect the Roguskhoi, circumstances offer."

The pacers, tall, rangy beasts, deep and narrow-chested, long and fine in the legs, sprang off down the road; the trap whirled after.

Etzwane glowered at Ifness from the corner of his eye. A strange man, for a fact; Etzwane had never seen another like him. Why should he want to inspect the Roguskhoi? There seemed no sensible reason for such an interest. If a Roguskhoi were dead and lying beside the road, Etzwane would pause to examine the corpse from natural curiosity; but to go about the business so purposefully—it seemed sheer lunacy!

Etzwane pondered the possibility that Ifness, for a fact, might be insane. The preoccupied placidity, the indifference to others, the bizarre predilections, all were suggestive of dementia. Still Ifness was nothing if not self-controlled; his appearance—spare, austere, otherwise nondescript save for the cropped white hair, the old-young face—seemed the very definition of sanity. Etzwane lost interest in the subject; he had other, more pressing concerns.

Ten miles they drove, up and down the rolling hills of Seamus. Along the road from the east came a man on a thrust-cycle wearing the red cap of invisibility. He rode at the best speed he could muster, lying flat on the pallet, buttocks surging and jerking as he kicked at the ratchet.

Ifness pulled the trap to a halt and watched the man's approach. A discourteous act, thought

Etzwane; the man wore red. The cyclist swerved to pass by. Ifness called him to a halt, to the man's displeasure.

"Why do you molest me? Have you no eyes in your head?"

Ifness ignored his agitation. "What is the news?"

"Dreadful news; don't stay me; I'm off to Canton Sable or beyond." He made as if to hump the cycle into motion once more; Ifness called out politely: "A moment, if you please. No danger is visible. From what are you fleeing?"

"From the Roguskhoi; what else? They burnt Salubra Village; another band pillaged the Chilites. For all I know they're close on my heels! Delay me no longer; if you're wise, you'll turn about and flee west at all speed!" The man thrust his cycle into motion and was gone along the road to Carbade.

Ifness turned to look at Etzwane. "Well, what now?"

"I must go to Bashon."

Ifness nodded and without further remark whipped up the pacers.

Etzwane leaned forward, heart in his mouth. Visions crossed before his eyes. He thought of florins wasted on drink, gifts to occasional sweethearts, unnecessary garments, his costly silver-mounted wood-horn. Frolitz thought him niggardly; he considered himself a wastrel. Vain regrets. The money was spent; the time was lost. The pacers, prime beasts, ran without fatigue; miles passed under the wheels. They entered Bastern; ahead appeared the shadow of Rhododendron Way. From behind the hill rose a column of smoke. As they entered Rhododendron Way, Ifness slowed the trap to a more cautious pace, inspecting the shadows under the trees, the berry coverts, the hillsides, with an alertness Etzwane had not noticed in him before. All seemed normal, save for the utter silence. The lavender-white sunlight lay in irregular sprinkles along the white dust; in the garden of the first cottage purple and magenta geraniums bloomed among spikes of lime-green ki. The door of the cottage hung askew. Across the threshhold lay the body of a man, face obliterated by a terrible blow. The girl who had lived in the cottage was gone.

A gap through the trees revealed the temple. Along the upper terraces a few Chilites moved slowly, tentatively, as if trying to convince themselves that they were alive. Ifness touched up the pacers; the trap whirled up the hill toward the temple. From the embers of the tannery and women's dormitory rose the column of smoke they had seen from far off. The temple and its conjoined structures seemed to be whole. Etzwane, standing up in the trap, looked all around. He saw no women, young or old.

Ifness halted the trap before the temple portico. From the terrace above a group of Chilites, haggard and uncertain, peered down.

Ifness called up: "What has happened?"

The Chilites stood like ghosts in their white robes. "Hello up there!" called Ifness with acerbity in his voice. "Can you hear me?"

The Chilites moved slowly back out of sight, as if toppling over backward, thought Etzwane.

Several minutes passed. The three suns performed their majestic gyrations across the sky.

The stone walls baked in the glare. Ifness sat without motion. Again, with sharper puzzlement, Etzwane wondered why Ifness troubled himself to such an extent.

The iron gates moved ajar and revealed a group of Chilites. He who had opened the gate was a round-faced young man, somewhat portly, with overlarge features, scant sandy hair, and a full sandy beard. Etzwane on the instant recognized Geacles Vonoble. Behind stood half a dozen other Chilites, and one among them was Osso Higajou.

Ifness spoke sharply, "What has occurred here?"

Osso said in a voice that rasped as if bitter phlegm choked his throat, "We are victims of the Roguskhoi. We have been pillaged; they have done us vast harm."

"How many were there in the band?"

"No less than fifty. They swarmed at us like savage beasts! They beat on our doors; they brandished weapons; they burnt our structures!"

"In the process of defending your women and your property, you doubtless inflicted many casualties?" inquired Ifness dryly.

The Chilites drew back in indignation; Geacles gave a contemptuous laugh. Osso said in a waspish voice, "We are nonviolent folk; we advocate peace."

"Did the abducted women defend themselves?" inquired Ifness.

"Yes, many of them; it did no good, and they violated their consciences in the process."

"They must suffer doubly in that case," Ifness agreed. "Why did you not shelter them in the temple?"

The Chilites surveyed him in calm silence, making no response.

Ifness asked again: "In regard to the Roguskhoi, what weapons did they carry?"

Geacles pulled at his beard, glanced off across the hillside. He spoke in a subdued voice: "They carried cudgels studded with spikes; these swung from their wrists. They wore scimitars at their belts, which they did not use."

"How long ago did they depart?"

"No more than an hour; they herded the women into a file; young and old, infants excepted; these they threw into the tannery vats. We are now bereft."

Etzwane could restrain himself no longer. "Which way did they go?"

Geacles stared at Etzwane, then turned and muttered to Osso, who came forward three quick steps.

Ifness, coldly polite, put the question a second time: "Which way did they go?"

"Up the Mirk Valley, the way they had come," said Geacles.

Osso pointed a finger at Etzwane. "You are the Pure Boy Faman Bougozonie who committed foul acts and fled."

"My name is Gastel Etzwane. I am the son of Dystar the druithine. My mother is the lady Eathre."

Osso spoke in a menacing voice: "Why did you come here?"

"I came to dissolve my mother's indenture."

Osso smiled. "We do not engage in such casual traffic."

"I carry an ordinance from the Faceless Man."

Osso grunted. Geacles said smoothly, "Why not? Pay us our money; the woman will be released to you."

Etzwane made no response. He turned to look up Mirk Valley where he had never ventured for fear of ahulphs. The women would walk at less than three miles an hour. The Roguskhoi had departed an hour since. Etzwane thought furiously. He looked toward the tannery: destroyed, burnt to the ground. The far sheds where chemicals and dyes were stored still stood. He turned to Ifness and spoke in a low voice: "Will you lend me the trap and the pacers? If I lose them, I will pay; I carry sixteen hundred florins."

"Why do you require the trap?"

"So that I may save my mother."

"How?"

"It depends upon Osso."

"I will lend you the trap. What are a pair of pacers, after all?"

Etzwane spoke to Osso: "The Roguskhoi are great wine-drinkers. Give me two large kegs of wine. I will convey them up the valley and deliver them."

Osso blinked in bewilderment. "You intend to assist their revelries?"

"I intend to poison them."

"What?" cried Geacles. "And so provoke another attack?"

Etzwane looked to Osso. "What do you say?"

Osso calculated. "You plan to deliver the wine in the trap?"

"I do."

"What will you pay for the wine? It is our ceremonial liquor; we have none other."

Etzwane hesitated. Time was too precious to be used haggling; still, if he offered generously, Osso would ask more. "I can only offer what it is worth, thirty florins a cask."

Osso gave Etzwane a cold glance. Ifness lounged indifferently against the trap. Osso said, "That is not enough."

Ifness said, "It is ample. Bring forth the wine."

Osso examined Ifness. "Who are you?"

Ifness looked unsmilingly off over the valley. Presently he said, "In due course the Faceless Man will move against the Roguskhoi. I will inform him of your refusal to cooperate."

"I have refused nothing," rasped Osso. "Give me your sixty florins, then go to the door of the storeroom."

Etzwane paid over the coins. Two casks of wine were rolled forth and loaded into the back of the trap. Etzwane ran over to the chemical storehouse, looked along the lines of jugs and packets. Which would serve his purpose best? He did not know.

Ifness entered the shed. He glanced along the shelf and selected a cannister. "This will serve best. It has no remarkable flavor and is highly toxic."

"Very well." They returned to the trap.

"I will be gone at least six hours," said Etzwane. "If possible, I will bring back the trap, but as to this——"

"I paid a large deposit for the use of the trap," said Ifness. "It is a valuable piece of equipment."

With compressed lips Etzwane brought forth his pouch. "Will two hundred florins suffice? Or as many as you wish, to sixteen hundred."

Ifness climbed into the seat. "Put away your

florins. I will come along to protect my interests."

Wordlessly Etzwane sprang aboard; the trap
moved off up Mirk Valley. From the terraces of
the temple the Chilites stood watching until the
trap passed from view.

Chapter 8

The road was little more than a pair of wheel tracks beside the Mirk River. To either side were flats overgrown with rich green bandocks, each plant raising a single pale blue spine that flicked at passing insects. Along the river grew willows, alders, clumps of stately dark blue miter-plants. Signs of the Roguskhoi were evident: odd articles of female clothing; on three occasions the corpses of old women, looking harried beyond their capacity; and in one dreary little heap, the corpses of six infants, evidently pulled from their mothers and dashed to the ground.

Ifness drove at the best pace the road allowed: The trap bounced, bumped, swung from side to side, but still moved three times the best possible speed of the Roguskhoi and the women.

Ifness asked after a few minutes, "Where does the road lead?"

"Up to Gargamet Meadow—that's what the Chilites call it. It's the plantation where they grow their galga bush."

"And how far to Gargamet Meadow?"

"Five or six miles from here, at a guess. I would expect the Roguskhoi to stop at Gargamet Meadow for the night."

Ifness pulled in the pacers. "We don't want to overtake them in this gully. Have you poisoned the wine?"

"I'll do so now." Etzwane climbed into the rear

of the trap and poured half of the cannister into each keg.

The suns passed behind the western slope; the valley began to grow dim. A sense of imminence pressed down on Etzwane; the Roguskhoi could not be too far ahead. Ifness drove with great caution; to blunder into a Roguskhoi rear guard would not serve their purposes. Ahead the road passed through a notch with tall coral-trees silhouetted on the sky at either side. Ifness stopped the cart; Etzwane ran ahead to reconnoiter. The road, passing through the notch, swung around a clump of purple-pear trees, then eased out upon a flat. To the left loomed a grove of dark bawberrys; to the right the galga plantation spread: sixty acres of carefully-tended vines. Beside the bawberry grove a pond reflected back the lavender sky; here the Roguskhoi marshaled their captives. They had just arrived; the women were still moving as the Roguskhoi directed with great roaring commands and sweeps of their huge arms.

Etzwane signaled back to Ifness, who brought the trap forward to the clump of purple-pears. With pinched nostrils Ifness looked across the flat. "We can't be too transparent in our scheme," he told Etzwane. "We must contrive natural movements."

Etzwane's nerves began to draw and grate. He spoke in a high-pitched, rasping voice: "Any minute they'll start in on the women! They can hardly contain themselves."

Indeed, the Roguskhoi now surrounded the women, making tremulous motions, surging toward the shrinking huddle, then drawing back.

Ifness inquired, "Can you ride a pacer?"

"I suppose so," said Etzwane. "I've never tried."

"We will drive across the meadow furtively, as if hoping to evade attention. As soon as they see us—then you must be quick, and I as well."

Etzwane, terrified but desperately resolved, nodded to Ifness's instructions. "Anything, anything. We must hurry!"

"Haste provokes disaster," chided Ifness. "We have just arrived; we must take account of every circumstance." He appraised and considered another ten seconds, then drove out on the edge of the meadow and turned toward the plantation, away from the bawberry grove. They moved in full view of the Roguskhoi, should one by chance remove his glance from the ashen-faced women.

They drove a hundred yards, attracting no attention; Ifness nodded in satisfaction. "It would seem now as if we are hoping to escape their notice."

"What if they don't see us?" asked Etzwane in a thin voice he hardly recognized as his own.

Ifness made no response. They drove another fifty yards. From the Roguskhoi came a yell, hoarse yet wild, with a peculiar crazy timber that started up the hairs behind Etzwane's neck.

"They have seen us," said Ifness in a colorless voice. "Be quick now." He jumped down from the cart with no undue haste and unsnapped the traces from one of the pacers; Etzwane fumbled with the straps of the other pacer. "Here," said Ifness, "take this one. Climb upon its back and take the reins."

The pacer jerked at the unaccustomed weight and lowered its head.

"Ride for the road," said Ifness. "Not too fast."

Twenty of the Roguskhoi lumbered across the

meadow, eyes distended, arms flailing and pumping: A fearful sight. Ifness ignored them. He snapped loose the traces on the second pacer, cut short the reins, tied them deliberately, jumped upon the pacer's back. Then, kicking it in the ribs, he sent the beast loping after Etzwane.

The Roguskhoi, sighting the casks, forgot the fugitives; with hardly a pause in their stride they lifted the tongue of the trap; cavorting in particularly grotesque fashion, they drew it back across the meadow.

In the shadow of the purple-pears Ifness and Etzwane halted the pacers. "Now," said Ifness, "we must wait."

Etzwane made no reply. The Roguskhoi, abandoning the women, swarmed around the trap. The casks were broached; the Roguskhoi drank with hoarse bellows of approval.

In a strained voice Etzwane asked, "How long before the poison acts?"

"So much poison would kill a man within minutes. I hopefully assume that the Roguskhoi metabolism is similar."

The two watched the encampment. The wine had been totally consumed. With no evidence either of sickness or intoxication the Roguskhoi turned upon the women. Each rushed into the whimpering group and without regard for age or condition seized a female and began to tear away clothing.

Ifness said: "The moment has come."

Several of the Roguskhoi had stopped short to gaze uncomprehendingly at the ground. Slowly they touched their abdomens, their throats, drew their fingers across their naked red scalps. Others displayed similar symptoms; the women, gasping and sobbing, crawled away in random directions like insects poured from a bottle. The Roguskhoi commenced to writhe, to dance a strange, slow ballet; they raised a crooked leg, clamped knee against abdomen, hopped, then repeated the antic on the opposite leg. Their faces sagged, their mouths hung pendulous.

Suddenly, in terrible rage, one cried out a word incomprehensible to Etzwane. The others shouted the same word in grotesque despair. One of the Roguskhoi dropped to his knees and slowly crumpled to the ground. He began to work his arms and legs like a beetle turned on its back. Certain of the women who had almost reached the bawberry grove began to run. The movement stimulated the warriors to frenzy. Staggering, reeling, they lurched in pursuit, flailing with their bludgeons. Screaming, sobbing, the women ran this way and that; the Roguskhoi jumped among them; the women were caught and beaten to the ground.

The Roguskhoi began to topple, one after the other. Ifness and Etzwane stepped out upon the meadow; the last Roguskhoi erect noticed their presence. He snatched out his scimitar and hurled it. "Take care!" cried Ifness, and sprang nimbly back. The scimitar whirled murderously through the air but curved to the side and slashed into the dirt. With renewed dignity Ifness once more stepped forward, while the last Roguskhoi fell to the ground.

Ifness said, "The trap appears to be unharmed. Let us reclaim it."

Etzwane looked at him, face blank with horror. He made a sound in his throat, moved forward a step, then halted. The features of the women had been blurred—by motion, by distance. Almost all he had known. Some had been kind, some had been beautiful; some had laughed, some had been sorrowful. With his poison he had contributed to the massacre, still—what else, what else?

"Come along," said Ifness brusquely. "Lead your pacer." He marched across the meadow, never troubling to look back.

Etzwane followed sluggishly, forcing his feet to move.

Arriving at the Roguskhoi camp, Ifness inspected the bodies with fastidious interest. The Roguskhoi still made small movements: twitches, jerks, clenched digging with the fingers. Etzwane forced himself to look here and there. He noticed the body of his sister Delamber: dead. Her face had been smashed almost beyond recognition; Etzwane recognized first the red-gold glints of her hair. He wandered across the field. There was Eathre. He fell down on his knees beside her and took her hands. He thought she still lived, though blood oozed from both her ears. He said, "It is Etzwane: your son Mur. I am here. I tried to save you, but I failed."

Eathre's lips moved. "No," he thought to hear her say, "you didn't fail. You saved me . . . Thank you, Mur . . ."

Etzwane dragged branches and boughs from the bawberry woods, stacked them high; he had no spade to dig a grave. He placed the bodies of Eathre and Delamber on the pyre and placed more branches to lean around and over. He needed much wood; he made many trips.

Ifness had been otherwise occupied. He har-

nessed the restive pacers to the trap and repaired
the reins. Then he turned his attention to the
Roguskhoi. He examined them closely, with
frowning concentration. To Etzwane they seemed
much alike: muscular, massive creatures, a
head taller than the average man, with a skin
hard and sleek as copper. Their features, which
might have been hewn with an axe, were con-
torted and twisted, like those of a demon-mask:
probably the effect of the poison. They grew no
hair on head or body; their costumes were almost
pitifully meager: black leather crotch-pieces, a
belt from which hung their bludgeons and scimitars. Ifness took up one of the scimitars and examined the gleaming metal with interest. "No
product of Shant here," he mused. "Who forged
such metal?"

Etzwane had no answer; Ifness placed the
scimitar in the back of the trap. The cudgels
likewise interested him. The handles were sea-
soned hardwood, eighteen inches long; the heads
were iron balls studded with two-inch points:
terrible weapons.

Etzwane finally completed the pyre and set it
afire on four sides. Flame licked up into the air.

Ifness had taken upon himself a grisly investigation. With his knife he had slit open the abdomen of one of the Roguskhoi. Blackish-red in-
testines rolled out; Ifness moved them aside
with a stick; with nostrils fastidiously pinched, he
continued his inspection of the creature's organs.

Dusk had come to the meadow. The pyre burnt
high. Etzwane did not care to tarry longer. He
called to Ifness: "Are you ready to leave?"

"Yes," said Ifness. "I have one small further
task."

While Etzwane watched in utter astonishment, Ifness selected the corpses of six women; deftly cutting off the battered heads, he took the six torcs. Going to the pond, he washed torcs, knife, and hands and returned to where Etzwane stood by the trap, wondering as to Ifness's sanity and his own.

Ifness seemed brisk and cheerful. He stood back to watch the flames from the pyre lick high into the gathering darkness. "It is time to go," said Ifness.

Etzwane climbed into the seat of the trap. Ifness turned the pacers across the meadow. Etzwane suddenly signaled him to a halt. Ifness pulled up the pacers; Etzwane jumped to the ground. He ran back to the pyre, extracted a burning brand. This he carried to the galga plantation and fired the foliage, which was dense, dry, heavy with resin. Flames surged up through clouds of black smoke. In grim delight Etzwane stood back to watch; then he ran back to the trap.

Ifness had no comment to make; Etzwane was unable to sense either approval or disapproval but did not care particularly.

Leaving the meadow, they halted and looked back at the two fires. The galga patch lit the sky; the pyre glowed ruby red. Etzwane turned away, blinking. The fires were the past; when the fires died to ashes, the past would be gone.

Down the dark valley moved the trap, by the light of the Skiaffarilla. The shuffle of hoofs, the creak of harness, and the soft scrape of wheels were the only sounds; they magnified the silence. Once or twice Etzwane looked back to watch the red glow slowly fading. At last he could see it no more; the sky was dark. He turned in the seat and gazed somberly ahead.

In a quiet and formal voice Ifness asked, "Now that you have studied the Roguskhoi, what is your opinion?"

Etzwane said, "They must be mad or demon-possessed. In a sense they are pitiable. But they must be destroyed."

Ifness said reflectively, "I find myself in agreement with you. The cantons of Shant are highly vulnerable. The Chilites must now change beyond recognition or disappear."

Etzwane tried to see Ifness's face in the starlight. "You can't believe this is unfortunate?"

"I regret the passing of any unique organism; there has never been such a human adaptation before in all the history of the race; there may never be again."

"What of the Roguskhoi: I suppose you'd be sorry to see them destroyed!"

Ifness gave a small, quiet laugh. "Rather than the Roguskhoi themselves, I fear what they may represent. To such an extent that I have been forced to compromise my principles."

"I don't understand you," said Etzwane shortly.

Ifness said in a grave voice, "As you know, I travel here and there across Shant, according to the urgencies of my profession. I see many circumstances, some happy, others grievous, but by the very nature of my affairs I may never involve myself."

Into Etzwane's mind came the memory of his first encounter with Ifness. "Not even to help a small boy escape the cannibal ahulphs?"

Ifness turned to peer through the darkness. "You were that boy?"

"Yes."

Ifness was silent for several minutes. Then he said, "You have a dark and brooding streak in your nature which persuades you against your best interests. By resurrecting an episode ten years old you risk offending me; what benefit do you derive?"

Etzwane spoke in a detached voice. "I have long resented that placid man who was willing to let me die. To express myself is a relief and a pleasure. I suppose that is the benefit which you asked about. I don't care a fig whether or not you are offended." Now that he had started talking, he found that he could not stop. "All that I have hoped and worked for is gone. Who is to blame? The Roguskhoi. Myself. The Faceless Man. The Chilites. All of us are to blame. I should have come sooner. I try to excuse myself: I had insufficient funds, I could not have anticipated the Roguskhoi raid. Still, I should have come sooner. The Roguskhoi—they are mad things; I am glad I poisoned them; I would gladly poison the entire race. The Chilites, whom you mourn: I don't care a fig for them, either. The Faceless Man: There is another matter! We have trusted him to protect us; we pay his imposts; we wear his torc; we follow, as we must, his edicts. To what end? Why has he not acted against the Roguskhoi? It is disheartening, to say the least!"

"And to say the most?"

Etzwane only shook his head. "Why did you cut open the Roguskhoi?"

"I was curious as to their physiology."

Etzwane gave a laugh that held a shrill note of wildness. He cut the laugh short. For a period there was silence. The trap moved down the starlit valley. Etzwane had no notion of how far they had come, how far they must go. He asked another question: "Why did you take the torcs?"

Ifness sighed. "I had hoped you would not ask that question. I cannot provide you a satisfactory answer."

"You have many secrets," said Etzwane.

"All of us keep covert certain areas of ourselves," said Ifness. "You yourself for instance: you have evinced dissatisfaction with the Faceless Man, but you do not reveal your further intentions."

"They are not secret," said Etzwane. "I shall go to Garwiy; I shall buy a Purple Petition; I shall argue my views with as much clarity as possible. Under the circumstances the Faceless Man must take notice."

"One would think so," Ifness concurred. "But let us assume the contrary. What, then?"

Etzwane squinted sidewise at the stiff yet casual silhouette against the blazing Skiaffarilla. "Why should I trouble myself with remote eventualities?"

"I agree that overplanning sometimes limits spontaneity," said Ifness. "Still, when there are but two cases of equal probability, it is wise to consider contingencies in both directions."

"I have ample time to form my plans," said Etzwane shortly.

Chapter 9

In the dead middle of the night they came down out of Mirk Valley. A few dim lights flickered from the terraces of the temple; a breeze brought the sweet-acrid whiff of galga mingled with vile odors of charred wood and hides.

"The Chilites will worship Galexis until their drug runs out," remarked Ifness. "Then they must cry after a new goddess."

They passed into Rhododendron Way, an avenue breathless and dark, haunted by remembered sounds. The foliage was black overhead, the road a white glimmer below. The cottages stood with doors ajar, offering shelter and rest; neither of the two suggested a halt. They continued on through the night.

Dawn came as a glorious cascade of orange and violet across the east; as Sasetta curveted into the sky, the trap entered Carbade. The pacers walked slowly, heads drooping, considerably more weary than the men.

Ifness drove directly to the hostler's and relinquished the conveyance; the torcs and the weapons he wrapped into a parcel and tucked into his jacket.

Etzwane would return westward; at Brassei Ifness had stated his destination to be in the east. Etzwane said somewhat ponderously, "We go our different ways. I can't ignore the fact that you have helped me a great deal. I give you thanks, and I must say that I leave you in a better spirit than I did on a previous occasion. So then, Ifness, I bid you farewell."

Ifness bowed courteously. "Farewell to you."

Etzwane turned and strode across the square to the balloon-way depot. Ifness followed in a more leisurely fashion.

At the ticket-seller's window Etzwane said in a crisp voice, "I want passage by the first balloon to Garwiy." As he paid the fee, he became conscious of Ifness standing behind him and gave a curt nod that Ifness returned. Ifness went to the wicket and arranged balloon passage for himself.

The balloon south to Junction would not arrive at Carbade for another hour; Etzwane paced back and forth, then crossed the square to a food-vender's stall where he found Ifness. Etzwane took his meal to a table nearby, as did Ifness, after murmuring a conventional excuse to Etzwane.

The two ate in silence. Etzwane, finishing, returned to the depot, followed somewhat later by Ifness.

The slot began to sing: a thin, high-pitched whirring that told of the approaching dolly. Five minutes later the balloon came trembling and swaying down to the loading platform. Etzwane rose to his feet, leaving Ifness looking pensively from the depot window; he entered the gondola and settled himself upon the bench. Ifness came in behind him and took a seat directly opposite. Etzwane could ignore his presence no longer. "I thought you were continuing east."

"An urgent matter takes me elsewhere," said Ifness.

"To Garwiy?"

"To Garwiy."

The balloon rose into the air; riding the fresh morning wind, it slid up the slot toward Junction.

During Etzwane's time Frolitz had taken his troupe to Garwiy but seldom, and only for short periods; the folk of Garwiy preferred entertainments more dramatic, more frivolous, more urbane. Etzwane nonetheless found Garwiy a fascinating place, if only for the marvel and grace of its vistas.

In all the human universe there was no city like Garwiy, which was built of glass—blocks, slabs, prisms, cylinders of glass: purple, green lavender, blue, rose, dark scarlet.

Among the original exiles from Earth had been twenty thousand Chama Reya, a cult of aestheticians. On Durdane they vowed to build the most magnificent city the race had yet known, and so dedicated themselves. The first Garwiy persisted seven thousand years, dominated in turn by the Chama Reya, the Architectural Corporation, the Director Dynasties, the transitional Superdirectors, and finally the Purple Kings. Each century brought new marvels to Garwiy, and it seemed that the goal of each Purple King was to daunt the memory of the past and stupefy the future. King Cluay Pandamon erected an arcade of nine hundred crystal columns sixty feet tall, supporting a prismatic glass roof. King Pharay Pandamon ordained a market pavilion of startling ingenuity. In a circular lake curved glass hulls were joined to form twelve floating concentric rings, each twenty feet wide, separated by bearings so that each ring floated free of those to either side. On these floating ways merchants and craftsmen established a bazaar, each booth isolated from its neighbor by a panel of colored glass. In a subsurface way around the lake, a hundred bullocks pulled the outside ring into slow rotation, which, through the agency of the water surrounding the hulls, gradually impelled the inner rings to rotations. Every six hours the bullocks reversed the rotational direction of the outer ring, and presently the rings all rotated at various speeds in different directions, presenting a succession of shifting colors and shadows: this the market bazaar built by King Pharay Pandamon.

During the reign of King Jorje Shkurkane, Garwiy reached its peak. The slopes of the Ushkadel glittered with palaces; at the Jardeen docks glass ships unloaded the wares of the world: fibers, silks, and membranes from North Shant, the meat-products of Palasedra, salts and oxides from the mines of Caraz for the production of glass. All sixty-two cantons contributed to the glory of Garwiy; the Pandamon Bailiff was a familiar sight in the far corners of Shant. During King Kharene's unlucky reign, the south revolted; the Palasedran Eagle-Dukes crossed the Great Salt Bog to spark the Fourth Palasedran War, which terminated the Pandamon Dynasty.

During the Sixth Palasedran War Palasedran bombardiers established themselves on the Ushkadel Ridges, from where they were able to lob air-mines into the old city. Fountain after fountain of antique glass spurted high into the sunlight. At last the Warlord Viana Paizifume launched his furious uphill assault, which subsequently became the substance of legend. With his cataphracts destroyed, his Elite Pikes dazed and leaderless, his Glass Darts cramped against the base of the cliff, Paizifume destroyed the Palasedran host with a horde of crazed ahulphs, daubed with tar, set afire and directed up the Ushkadel. Victory was a poor exchange for Garwiy shattered; the deed brought the Palasedrans a permanent legacy of distrust and bitterness.

Viana Paizifume, from Canton Glirris on the east coast, refused to allow another Pandamon upon the Purple Throne and called a conclave of the cantons to form a new government. After three weeks of bickering and caprice, Paizifume's patience was exhausted. Mounting to the podium, he indicated a platform on which a screen had been arranged.

"Beyond that screen," decreed Paizifume, "sits your new ruler. I will not tell you his name; you will know him only by his edicts, which I shall enforce. Do you understand the virtue of this arrangement? When you do not know your ruler, you will be unable to plot, wheedle, or suborn. Justice at last is possible."

Did the first Faceless Man actually stand behind the screen? Or had Viana Paizifume invented an invisible *alter ego*? No one knew then or ever. However, when at last Paizifume was assassinated, the plotters were immediately apprehended, sealed into glass balls and suspended on a cable running between a pair of spires. For a thousand years the balls hung like baubles until one by one they were struck by lightning and destroyed.

For a period the Faceless Man enforced his commands by means of a coercive corps, which gradually assumed improper prerogatives and stimulated a revolt. The Conservative Counsel quelled the revolt, disbanded the Coercive Corps, and restored order. The Faceless Man appeared before the counsel in armor of black glass, with a black glass helmet to conceal his identity. He demanded and was conceded greater power and greater responsibility. For twenty years the total energies of Shant were expended in the perfection of the torc system. The Magenta Edict decreed torcs for all and stimulated further strife: the Hundred Years War, which ended only when the last citizen had been clamped into his torc.

Garwiy never regained its Pandamon magnificence but still was reckoned the first wonder of Durdane. There were towers of blue glass, spires of purple glass, green glass domes, prisms and pillars, walls of clear glass glinting and glittering in the sunlight. At night colored lamps illuminated the city: green lamps behind blue and purple glass, pink lamps behind blue glass.

The palaces up the Ushkadel still housed the patricians of Garwiy, but these were a far cry from the flamboyant grandees of the Pandamon Era. They drew their income from country estates, from shipping, from the laboratories and workshops where torcs, radios, glow-bulbs, a few other electronic devices, were assembled, using components produced elsewhere in Shant: monomolecule conductor strands, semiorganic electron-control devices, magnetic cores of sintered ironweb, a few trifles of copper, gold, silver, lead, for connections and switches. No technician comprehended the circuits he used; whatever the original degree of theoretical knowledge, it now had become lore: a mastery of techniques rather than of principles. The workshops and factories were located in the industrial suburb Shranke on the Jardeen River; the workers lived nearby in pleasant cottages among gardens and orchards.

This, then, was Garwiy: a metropolis of considerable area but no great population, a place of entrancing beauty enhanced by antiquity and the weight of history.

The people of Garwiy were unique—hyper-civilized, sensitive to all varieties of aesthetic distinction but not themselves particularly creative. The Aesthetic Society, with a membership of patricians from the Ushkadel, administered civic functions, which the ordinary folk of Garwiy found right and proper. The patricians had the money; it was right that they should accept the responsibilities. The typical citizen felt no resentment toward the patricians; he was equal before the law. If by dint of cleverness or energy he acquired a fortune and bought a palace, he was taken into the Aesthetic Society as a matter of course. After two or three generations as parvenus, his descendants might regard themselves as Aesthetes in their own right. This typical citizen was a complicated person: suave and civil, vivacious, fickle, frivolous, and somewhat brittle. He was voluptuous but critical; complacent but demanding; fashion-conscious but amused by eccentricity. He was gregarious but introverted; knowledgeable regarding every green facet and purple glint of his wonderful city, current with the latest entertainments, uninterested in the rest of Shant. He was not deeply moved by music and had no great patience with the traditions of the druithines or the musical troupes; he preferred facetious ballads, songs with topical ref-

erences, entertainers with eccentric antics: in
short, all the manifestations detested by the mu-
ician.

He regarded his torc as a necessary evil and
occasionally made a satirical reference to the
Faceless Man, for whom he felt a half-contemp-
tuous awe. Somewhere along the Ushkadel the
Faceless Man reputedly lived in a palace; the
question of his identity was a constant titillation
for the man of Garwiy. He seldom if ever exercised his right of petition; this facility was re-
served for the outlander, whom Garwiy folk liked
to consider a yokel. He had heard mention of the
Roguskhoi and perhaps wondered at their peculiar habits, but his interest went little further.
To the Garwiy man the wildlands of the Hwan
were almost as remote as the center of Caraz.

The suns toppled south toward the winter sol-
stice; Durdane at the same time entered that
sector of its orbit where the suns occulted: a
situation intensifying seasonal contrasts. Cold air
from Nimmir brought autumnal winds to the
north of Shant.

The balloon *Shostrel*, leaving Angwin, spun
down the Great Transverse at extraordinary
speeds, out of the Wildlands into Shade, then
Fairlea, and past Brassei Junction where Etzwane turned an expressionless glance west, to
where Frolitz presumably anticipated his early
arrival; through Cantons Conduce, Maiy, Wild
Rose, each jealous of its unique identity, and at
last into Canton Garwiy. Down the Vale of Silence
they veered at fifty miles an hour, along the line
of clear glass tablets, each encasing the monu-
mental effigy of a dynastic king. The poses were

identical; the kings stood with right feet slightly forward, forefingers pointing at the ground, the faces wearing somber, almost puzzled expressions, eyes staring ahead, as if in contemplation of an astounding future.

The wind-tender began to slacken his warps; the *Shostrel* sailed at an easier pace through the Jardeen Gap and into Garwiy Station. Brakes slowed the running dolly; a Judas was snatched to the guys so expertly that the balloon came to ground in a continuous even motion.

Etzwane alighted, followed by Ifness. With a polite nod Ifness walked off across the station plaza, to turn into Kavalesko Passway, which led under a tower of dark blue glass ribbed with water-blue pilasters, and into Kavalesko Avenue.* Etzwane shrugged and went his way.

Frolitz customarily made resort at Fontenay's Inn, north of the plaza, beside the Jardeen, where the management provided meals and lodging in return for a few evenings of music. To Fontenay's Inn Etzwane now betook himself. He called for stylus and paper and immediately set to work drafting the petition that he planned to submit on the following day.

Two hours later Etzwane finished the document. He gave it a final reading and could find no fault; it seemed clear and uncompromising, with no sacrifice of calm reason. It read:

> To the attention of the ANOME:
>   During my recent visit to the lowlands of the Hwan, in Canton Bastern, I observed

---

* The twelve avenues radiating from the Aesthetic Corporation Plaza were named for Chama Reya avatars.

the effects of a Roguskhoi raid upon the Chilite community Bashon. Considerable property damage occurred: a tannery and certain out-buildings were demolished. A large
number of women were abducted and subsequently killed under distressing circumstances.

It has become well known that the Wildlands of the Hwan are a haven for those
noxious savages, who therefore are free to
maraud and plunder at will. Each year they
wax both in numbers and audacity. It is my
opinion that all Roguskhoi now resident in
Shant should be destroyed by a stern and
unremitting effort. I suggest that a suitable
militia be recruited, trained, and armed.
Coincidentally, a study should be made of
the Roguskhoi, their habits, their preferred
resorts. When all is prepared, the militia,
using disciplined tactics, should penetrate
the Hwan, attack and expunge the Roguskhoi.

In broad outline, this is my petition. I
realize that I propose a major governmental
operation, but in my opinion such action
is necessary.

The time was late afternoon: too late to present
the petition. Etzwane crossed the Jardeen and
strolled through Pandamon Park where the north
wind sent autumn leaves scurrying past his feet.
He came to the Aeolian Hall, a musical instrument of pearl-gray glass three hundred feet long.
Wind collected by scoops was directed into a
plenum. The operator worked rods and keys to
let pent air move one, two, a dozen, or a hundred

from among the ten thousand sets of glass chimes.
A person who wandered the hall experienced
audible dimension, with sound coming from various directions: tinkling chords, whispers of
vaguely heard melody, thin, glassy shiverings,
the crystal-pure tones of the center gongs; hurried gusts racing the ceiling like ripples across a
pond; fateful chimes, pervasive and melancholy
as a buoy bell heard through the fog. On occasion
the entire ceiling would seem to burst into sound.

With the north wind at its full weight, Etzwane heard the hall at its best; at twilight he
crossed the river and dined in one of Garwiy's
splendid restaurants under a hundred pink and
lavender lamps—an experience he had hereto-
fore denied himself. The money he had hoarded
over the years: what was its purpose? It represented grief and futility; he would spend it as fast
as possible, frivol it away. His sober second self
quickly interposed a veto. He would do no such
thing. Money so hardly come by should not be
lightly dissipated. But tonight, at least, he would
enjoy his meal, and he forced himself to do so.
The courses were set before him by a pretty
waitress. Etzwane considered her with somber interest; she seemed amiable, with a mouth that
seemed always twitching on the verge of a smile.
He ate: the viands were prepared and presented
to perfection. The meal came to an end. Etzwane
wanted to talk to the waitress but felt too shy. In
any event she was of Garwiy, and he was an outlander; she would consider him quaint. He wondered as to the whereabouts of Frolitz, even of the
uncommunicative Ifness. In a fretful mood he returned to the inn. He looked into the tavern, which

was composed and quiet; no musicians were on hand. Etzwane took himself to bed.

In the morning he visited a haberdasher who fitted him out with new clothes: a white tunic with a high flaring collar, dark green breeches buckled at the ankles, black ahulph-leather boots with silver-wood clasps. He had never before owned an outfit so dashing. He was not altogether convinced that the figure in the carbon-fume mirror was himself. A barber trimmed his hair and shaved him with a glass razor. On a sudden impulse, as if to defy the jeers from his under-brain, he bought a rakish little cap with a medallion of colored glass. The image of himself in the mirror aroused a complicated emotion: disgust and wonder for his own folly, with a trace of ebullience, as if whatever flamboyant traits he had inherited from Dystar were pushing to make themselves felt. Etzwane shrugged and grimaced; he had spent the money; now he must wear the cap. He stepped out into the blazing lavender noon light; the glass of Garwiy flashed and glittered.

Etzwane walked slowly to the Corporation Plaza. To buy a five-hundred-florin petition, to assert his views, must bring him to the attention of the Faceless Man. Well, what, then? His concerns were valid; his petition was legal. They expressed honest anxiety; by his own assertion the Faceless Man was servant to the people of Shant!

Etzwane crossed the Corporation Plaza to the long, low structure of magenta glass where once before he had come. The front wall supported a panel of dull purple satin to which were pinned petitions and the Faceless Man's response. Twenty or thirty folk, in a variety of cantonal costumes, stood waiting at the five-florin window. They had come from every corner of Shant with their grievances; as they stood in line, they watched the passing folk of Garwiy with truculent expressions. Nearby were more dignified precincts for those earnest enough to buy a hundred-florin petition. At the far end of the building a door distinguished by a purple star opened into the chamber where the very wealthy or the very vehement bought petitions at a cost of five hundred florins.

Through this latter door marched Etzwane without slackening his stride.

The chamber was empty. He was the single petitioner. Behind the counter a man jumped to his feet. "Your wishes, sir?"

Etzwane brought forth his money. "A petition."

"Very well, sir. A matter of grave importance, no doubt."

"This is my opinion."

The clerk brought forth a magenta document, a pen, a dish of black ink; as Etzwane wrote, the clerk counted the money and prepared a receipt.

Etzwane indited his petition, folded it, tucked it into the envelope provided by the clerk, who, examining Etzwane's torc, noted the color code. "Your name, sir, if it please you?"

"Gastel Etzwane."

"Your native canton?"

"Bastern."

"Very good, sir; that is sufficient."

"When will I have my response?"

The clerk held wide his hands. "How can I answer? The Anome comes and goes; I know no more of his movements than you. In two or three days you might expect to find your response. It must be posted publicly like all the rest; no one may claim that the Anome performs private favors."

Etzwane went off somewhat less briskly than he had come. The deed was accomplished. He had done all he could; now he must wait upon the decision of the Faceless Man. He climbed a flight of green glass steps to a refreshment garden; the flowers, plants, fronds, and trees were all simulated of blue, green, white and scarlet glass. At a table overlooking the plaza he ate a dish of fruit and hard cheese. He ordered wine and was brought a goblet, slender and high as his lips, of pale cool Pelmonte. He felt dull, deflated. He even felt somewhat absurd. Had he been too bombastic? The Faceless Man surely understood every aspect of the problem; the petition would seem brash and callow. Etzwane glumly sipped his wine. Five hundred florins gone. For what? Expiation of guilt? So that was it. This flinging down of five hundred florins on a useless petition was the way he punished himself. Five hundred hard-earned florins!

Etzwane compressed his lips. He rubbed his forehead with his fingertips. What was done was done. At all events the Faceless Man's reply would provide information regarding counter-Roguskhoi measures now in progress.

Etzwane finished his wine and returned to Fontenay's Inn. He found the proprietor in the pot-room with a trio of cronies. He had been testing his own merchandise and had reached a difficult and captious state.

Etzwane asked politely, "Who plays the music here of evenings?"

The proprietor turned his head to survey Etzwane from head to toe; Etzwane regretted the expensive new clothes. In his old garments he looked the part of a traveling musician.

The proprietor responded curtly: "At the moment, no one."

"In that case I wish to apply for the chair."

"Aha. What are your abilities?"

"I am a musician. I often play the khitan."

"A budding young druithine, it seems."

"I do not present myself in such terms," replied Etzwane.

"A singer, then, with three chords and as many bogus dialects?"

"I am a musician, not a singer."

One of the cronies, seeing how the wind blew, held up his goblet and looked through the glass at the contents. "New wine is thin; old wine is rich."

"My own opinion exactly," said the proprietor. "A new musician knows too little, has felt too little; remember the great Aladar Szantho? He secluded himself fourteen years. Now, with no reflection upon either your aptitudes or potentialities, how could you interest a mature and knowledgeable company?"

"You will never know until you hear me."

"You refuse to be daunted? Very well, you shall play. I pay nothing unless you attract custom into the tavern, which I doubt."

"I expect no pay," said Etzwane, "other than my board and lodging."

"I can't even agree to that until I hear you. Garwiy is not a city which takes to outland music. If you could hypnotize toads or recite lewd verse or sing topical ballads or roll your eyes in opposite circles, that is another matter."

"I can only play music," said Etzwane. "My fee, if any, I will leave to your generosity. Is there a khitan on the premises?"

"You will find one or two such in the cupboard yonder."

Three days passed. Etzwane played in the pot-room, well enough to amuse the customers and satisfy the proprietor. He attempted no bravura and used the rattle-box with a delicate elbow.

On the third night, with the time growing late, the mood came upon him, and he struck the idle chords of the druithine commencing a reverie. He played a reflective melody and a minor retrospect. Music is the result of experience, he thought; he had had sufficient experience to be a musician. Admittedly some of his emotions were raw, and some of his chords were played with his knee too hard against the brilliancy lever. The awareness of this came to Etzwane; he changed, almost in midphrase, to soft, quiet passages. He noticed that the company had become attentive. Before he had been playing in an abstraction; now he felt self-conscious. Modulating into a set of conventional chords, he finished. He was afraid to raise his eyes and look out over the company. Might they have felt what he felt? Or were they smiling at his excesses? He put down the instrument and stepped from the chair.

To confront Frolitz. Who faced him with a queer half smile. "The sublime young druithine! Who performs his fantastic surprises at Fontenay's while his master, poor doddering old Frolitz, prays for his return at Brassei."

"I can explain everything," said Etzwane.

"Your mother is well, I hope?"

"She is dead."

" 'Dead' is a sour word," said Frolitz. He scratched his nose, drank from his mug, looked over his shoulder. "The troupe is here. Shall we play music?"

On the following morning Etzwane (again wearing his new garments) went to the Corporation Plaza and across to the Office of Petitions. To the left, gray cards gave answers to the five-florin petitions: adjudications of petty disputes, actions for damage, complaints against local restrictions. In the center, sheets of pale-green parchment, pinned to the board with emerald-glass cabochons, decided hundred-florin actions. At the far right documents of vellum with surrounding bands of black and purple announced responses to the five-hundred-florin petitions. Only three of these were posted on the board.

Etzwane could hardly restrain his strides as he crossed the plaza; the last few steps he almost ran.

He scanned the purple-and-black-bordered documents. The first read:

Lord Fiatz Ergold, having called for the ANOME'S intercession against the unusually harsh judgment rendered in Canton Amaze against his son, the Honorable Arlet, now may hear: The ANOME has requested a transcript of the proceedings and will study the case. The cited penalty appears disproportionate to the offense. Lord Fiatz Ergold however must know that an act merely vulgar or inopportune in one canton

is a capital offense in the next. The ANOME,
despite sympathy for Lord Fiatz Ergold, may
not in justice contravene local laws. However, if circumstances warrant, the ANOME
will pray for leniency.

The second read:

The gentlewoman Casuelda Adrio is advised that, notwithstanding her anger and
concern, the punishment she urges for the
man Andrei Simic will not beneficially re-
pair circumstances as they now exist.

The third read:

For the attention of the gentleman Gastel Etzwane and the other worthy folk who
have expressed concern for the Roguskhoi
bandits in the Wildlands of the Hwan, the
ANOME counsels a calm mien. These disgusting creatures will never dare to venture
down from the wilderness; their depreda-
tions are not likely to molest folk who make
it their business to avoid reckless exposure
of themselves and their properties.

Etzwane leaned forward, gaping in disbelief.
His hand went to his torc, the unconscious gesture of Shant folk when they reflected in regard
to the Faceless Man. He looked again. The state-
ment read exactly as it had originally. With a
trembling hand Etzwane reached to claw the
document from the display board. He restrained
himself. Let it stay. In fact . . .

He brought a stylus from his pocket; he wrote on the parchment:

> The Roguskhoi are murderous beasts! The Faceless Man says ignore them while they kill and plunder.
>
> The Roguskhoi infest our lands. The Faceless Man says keep out of their way.
>
> Viana Paizifume would have spoken differently.

Etzwane drew back from the board, suddenly abashed. His act was close to sedition, for which the Faceless Man had little patience. Anger flooded Etzwane again. Sedition, intemperance, insubordination. How could affairs be otherwise? Any man must be prompted to outrage by policy so bland and unresponsive! He looked around the plaza in trepidation and defiance. None of the folk nearby paid him any close attention. He noticed a man strolling slowly across the square, head bowed as if in cogitation. It was surely Ifness. He seemed not to have observed Etzwane, though he must have passed only thirty feet from the Petitioners' Board. On a sudden impulse Etzwane ran after him.

Ifness looked around without surprise. He seemed, thought Etzwane, even more placid than usual. Etzwane said, somewhat grimly, "I saw you pass, and I thought to pay my respects."

"Thank you," said Ifness. "How go your affairs?"

"Well enough. I am back with Master Frolitz; we play at Fontenay's Inn. You should come by and hear our music."

"A pleasant thought. Unluckily I fear I will be occupied. You seem to have altered your style." His glance indicated Etzwane's garments.

Etzwane scowled. "The clothes are nothing. A waste of money."

"And your petition to the Faceless Man: Have you had a response?"

Etzwane stared at him stonily, wondering if Ifness enjoyed subterfuge for its own sake; surely Ifness had noticed him at the board! He said carefully, "I bought the petition at a cost of five hundred florins. The answer has been posted. It is yonder."

He led Ifness to the board. Ifness read with his head thrust slightly forward. "Hmm," said Ifness. Then in a sharp voice, "Who wrote the remarks at the bottom of the sheet?"

"I did."

"*What!*" Ifness's voice was vibrant. Etzwane had never before seen him exercised. "Do you realize that in the building opposite a telescope is fixed on this board! You scribble your callow and irrelevant complaints, then stalk grandly over to implicate me. Do you realize that you are about to lose your head? Now we are both in danger."

Etzwane started to make a hot retort, but Ifness's gesture cut him short. "Act naturally; do not pose or posture. Cross to the Pomegranate Portal; continue slowly along. I must alter certain arrangements."

His head whirling, Etzwane crossed the plaza, moving with as natural a stride as he could muster. He looked toward the Aesthetic Corporation offices, from which, so Ifness averred, the board was telescopically monitored. The objective lens might well be that particularly lucid glass boss directly opposite the board. The Faceless Man hardly sat with his own eyes glued to the lens; a functionary no doubt kept vigil. The telescope would readily pick up the colors in Etzwane's torc; when he turned away, the man's curiosity would hold on him, and he would have observed the colloquy with Ifness.

If all were as Ifness declared. At least, thought Etzwane, he had startled Ifness from his supercilious calm.

He passed through the Pomegranate Portal, so called for festoons of dark scarlet fruit, into Serven Airo Way beyond.

Ifness caught up with him. "It is possible that your act went unnoticed," said Ifness. "But I cannot risk even one chance in ten."

Etzwane, still surly, said, "I understand none of your actions."

"Still, you would prefer not to lose your head?" asked Ifness in his most silky voice.

Etzwane gave a noncommittal grunt.

"Here is the situation," said Ifness. "The Faceless Man will shortly learn of your acts. He may well take your head; he has already taken the heads of three persons who have pushed too hard in this connection. I propose to prevent this. Next I intend to learn the identity of the Faceless Man. Then I will urge him to alter his policy."

Etzwane looked at Ifness in awe. "Can you do this?"

"I intend to try. You may be able to assist me."

"Why have you formed such plans? They are surprising!"

"Why did you file a five-hundred-florin petition?"

"You know my motives," said Etzwane stiffly.

"Exactly," said Ifness. "It gives me reason to trust in your participation. Walk faster. We are not being followed. Turn to the right at the Old Rotunda."

Passing from the city of glass, they walked a quarter mile north along the Avenue of the Thasarene Directors, into a lane shaded by tall blue-green hedges, through a gap to a small cottage of pale blue tile. Ifness unlocked the door, ushered Etzwane within. "Take off your jacket quickly."

Etzwane sulkily obeyed the instructions. Ifness indicated a couch. "Lie down, on your face."

Again Etzwane obeyed. Ifness wheeled over a table on which rested an assortment of tools. Etzwane rose from the couch to examine them; Ifness curtly told him to lie back. "Now, on your life, do not move."

Ifness switched on a bright light and clamped Etzwane's torc in a small vise. He slipped a metal strip between the torc and Etzwane's neck, then clipped a u-shaped device to the strip. He touched a button; the device set up a soft hum; Etzwane felt a tingle of vibration. "Electron flow is impeded," said Ifness. "It is safe to open your torc." With a spinning razor-sharp wheel he sliced the flexite of the torc along its seam. Putting the tool aside, he split the torc open, then, with a long-nose pliers, he drew forth a length of black soft stuff. "The dexax is removed." With a hooked rod he worked at the internal lock. The torc fell away from Etzwane's neck.

"You are no longer subject to the control of the Faceless Man," said Ifness.

Etzwane rubbed his neck, which felt thin-skinned and naked. Rising from the couch, he looked slowly from the torc to Ifness. "How did you learn to do this?"

"You will remember the torcs I salvaged on Gargamet Meadow. I studied these with great care." He indicated the interior of Etzwane's torc. "These are the coded receptors; this is a trigger mechanism. If a signal comes through from the Faceless Man, this fiber jerks to detonate the explosive. Off comes your head. This is the echo relay, which allows the Faceless Man to discover your whereabouts; it is now inoperative. These nodules I believe to be energy accumulators."

He stood frowning down at the device so long that Etzwane became restless and donned his tunic.

Ifness finally said, "If I were the Faceless Man, I might well suspect a cabal, of which Gastel Etzwane was not the most important member. I would not instantly take Etzwane's head, but I would use the echo circuit to locate him and investigate his activities."

"That seems reasonable enough," said Etzwane grudgingly.

"On this basis," said Ifness, "I will attach a signal to your torc; if and when the Faceless Man tries to locate you, we will be warned." He busied himself. "When he receives no return signal, he must assume that you have left the district, and we will have verified his interest in Gastel Etzwane. Above all, I do not wish to alarm him or put him on his guard."

Etzwane asked the question that long had been at the front of his mind. "What, in fact, are your wishes?"

"I hardly know," Ifness murmured. "My perplexity is greater than your own."

Sudden illumination came to Etzwane. "You are a Palasedran! You come to observe the work of the Roguskhoi!"

"Not true." Ifness, seating himelf on a couch, regarded Etzwane with a passionless gaze. "Like yourself, I wonder at the Roguskhoi and the Faceless Man's unconcern. Like yourself, I have been prompted to action. It is no less illicit for me than for you."

"What kind of action do you plan?" Etzwane asked cautiously.

"My first goal must be to identify the Faceless Man," said Ifness. "After that I will be guided by events."

"You claim not to be Palasedran," said Etzwane. "Nevertheless, this remains a possibility."

"My conduct in Mirk Valley was that of a Palasedran?"

Etzwane reflected upon Ifness's action. In no respect had Palasedran interests been advanced, or so it would seem. And the tools on the table: marvelous things! Of shining metal, of substances to which he could put no name—but not Palasedran. "If you are not Palasedran, what are you? Certainly no man of Shant."

Ifness leaned back on the couch, an expression of intense boredom on his face. "With churlish persistence you press for information I clearly do not wish to extend. Since your cooperation now becomes useful, I am forced to make certain disclosures. You have discerned that I am not a man of Shant. I am, in fact, an Earthman, a Fellow of the Historical Institute. Are you any the wiser?"

Etzwane surveyed him with a fierce gaze. "Earth is a real place?"

"Very real indeed."

"Why are you here on Shant?"

Ifness spoke in a patient voice. "The folk who came to Durdane nine thousand years ago were secretive and eccentric; they marooned themselves and sank their spaceships in the Purple Ocean. On Earth Durdane is long forgotten—except by the Historical Institute. I am the latest in a succession of Fellows resident upon Durdane—and possibly the first to ignore the First Law of the Institute: Fellows may never interfere in the affairs of the worlds they study. We are organized as a fact-gathering association, and we so restrict ourselves. My conduct in regard to the Faceless Man is absolutely illicit; in the purview of the Institute I am a criminal."

"Why, then, did you concern yourself?" Etzwane demanded. "Because of the Roguskhoi raids?"

"My motives need not concern you. Your interests, so far as they go, are concurrent with mine; I do not care to be more explicit."

Etzwane ran his hand through his hair and sank back down upon the couch opposite to that on which Ifness sat. "These are great surprises." He warily studied Ifness. "Are there other Earthmen on Durdane?"

Ifness replied in the negative. "The Historical Institute spreads its personnel thin."

"How do you move between here and Earth?"

"Again, this is information I prefer to keep to myself."

Before Etzwane could make an irritated reply,

his torc produced a sharp buzzing sound. Ifness jumped to his feet; in one long stride he was at the torc. The buzzing stopped, leaving a silence that had a weighty and sinister quality of its own. Somewhere, thought Etzwane, the Faceless Man had turned away from his instruments frowning.

"Excellent!" Ifness declared. "The Faceless Man is interested in you. We will persuade him to reveal himself."

"All very well," said Etzwane, "but how?"

"A tactical exercise, which we will discuss presently. At the moment I wish to resume the business which your presence in the Plaza interruped. I was about to dine."

The two returned to the Corporation Plaza; here they kept to the peripheral arcade, beyond the purview of the observer in the Corporation Center. Etzwane looked toward the Office of Petitions; the purple-and-black-bordered document was no longer to be seen. He informed Ifness of the fact.

"Another evidence of the Anome's sensitivity," said Ifness in an abstracted voice. "Our work will be the easier on this account."

"How so?" demanded Etzwane, ever more irritated by Ifness's condescension.

Ifness looked sidewise with raised eyebrows and spoke in a patient voice: "We must induce the Faceless Man to reveal himself. A quail cannot be seen until it moves; so with the Faceless Man. We must generate a situation which he will wish to inspect in his own person, rather than relying upon his Benevolences. The fact of his sensitivity makes such a reaction more likely."

Etzwane gave a sardonic grunt. "Just so. What situation do we generate?"

"It is a matter we must discuss. First, let us dine."

They seated themselves in the loggia of the Old Pagane Restaurant; their meal was set before them. Ifness stinted himself nothing. Etzwane, unsure whether or not he might be required to pay his own score, dined less lavishly. In the end, however, Ifness laid down money for both meals and leaned back to sip the dessert wine. "Now, to our business. The Faceless Man returned a polite response to your five hundred florins and in fact evinced interest only when you noted your dissatisfaction. This calibrates one of our parameters."

Etzwane wondered where all this was leading.

Ifness mused: "We must act within bounds of Garwiy law, to give the Aesthetic Corporation no pretext for action. Perhaps we will offer an informative lecture on the Roguskhoi and promise startling revelations. The faceless Man has demonstrated his concern in regard to this subject; in all probability he will be interested enough to attend."

Etzwane agreed that such a contingency was possible. "But who will give such a lecture?"

"That is a matter to be carefully considered," said Ifness. "Let us return to the cottage. Again I must modify your torc so that it becomes a tool of aggression rather than a mere warning device."

In the cottage once more, Ifness worked two hours on the modification of Etzwane's torc. At last he completed his work. A pair of inconspicuous wires now led to a coil of fifty turns tied down upon a square of stiff fiber board. "This is a directional antenna," said Ifness. "You will wear

the coil under your shirt. Warning signals inside
the torc will notify you when an attempt is being made either to locate you or to take your
head. By turning, you will maximize the signals
and thus determine their direction. Allow me now
to place the torc around your neck."

Etzwane submitted without enthusiasm. "It
seems," he grumbled, "that I am to function as
bait."

Ifness allowed himself a frosty smile. "Something of the sort. Now listen carefully. The explosive impulse you will feel as a vibration against
the back of your neck. The locator pulse will be
received as a vibration at the right side. In either
case, turn until you maximize the vibration. The
source will then be directly in front of you."

Etzwane nodded grimly. "And what of you?"

"I will carry a similar device. With luck we
should be able to strike a fix upon our subject."

"And what if we are unlucky?"

"This, to be frank, is my expectation. Such
facile success is too much to hope for. We may
startle our quail on this occasion, but other quail
may move as well and so confuse us. But I will
carry my camera; we will at least have an exact
record of the occasion."

Chapter 10

At those places throughout Garwiy designated for the display of public announcements appeard large placards printed in brown and black on white paper with a yellow border: colors to signify dire and fateful import, with overtones of the sensationally macabre.

The ROGUSKHOI EXPOSED!
Who are these horrid savages who ravage and rape, who torment our land? Where do they come from? What is their plan?
AN ANONYMOUS ADVENTURER JUST RETURNED FROM THE HWAN WILL REVEAL STARTLING FACTS AND EVEN MORE STARTLING SUSPICIONS. WHO SHARES THE BLAME FOR THIS INFESTATION? YOU WILL HEAR AN AMAZING ACCUSATION!

MIDAFTERNOON KYALISDAY
AT THE PUBLIC PAVILION
IN PANDAMON PARK

On a hundred bulletin boards the placards were posted, and even the folk of Garwiy took notice, reading the placards once, twice, a third time. Ifness was pleased with the effect. "The Faceless Man will not ignore this. Yet we give neither him nor the Corporation cause to interfere."

Etzwane said sourly, "I'd rather that you were the 'anonymous adventurer.' "

Ifness laughed—in high good humor. "What? The talented Gastel Etzwane uncomforable before an audience? What happens when you play one of your instruments?"

"That is different."

"Possibly so. But as the 'anonymous adventurer' I could not use my camera. You have memorized the material?"

"As much as needs be," growled Etzwane. "In all candor, I dislike acting as your cat's-paw. I do not care to be seized by the Discriminators* and clapped off to Stonebreakers' Island while you dine on pomfret and inger eggs at the Old Pagane."

"Unlikely," said Ifness. "Not impossible but unlikely."

Etzwane merely grunted. As an "anonymous adventurer" he wore a bulky cape of black fur, square and wide across the shoulders, with sand-colored breeches and black boots: the garments of a Canton Shkoriy mountaineer. The medallion of his torc showed at his neck; the designation "musician" was not at odds with the role of "adventurer." Slender, taut, his face keen and quick-featured, Gastel Etzwane cut a gallant figure in the mountaineer's costume; insensibly it affected his stride, his mannerisms, his mode of thought. He had become in fact the "anonymous adventurer." Ifness, wearing dark gray trousers, a loose white shirt, a soft gray jacket, was as usual. If Ifness felt any emotion, he gave no indication;

---

* *Avistioi:* literally, "nice discriminators": the constabulary of the Aesthetic Corporation.

Etzwane found it difficult to control his nervousness.

They arrived at Pandamon Park.

"A half hour to the midafternoon chime," said Ifness. "A fair number of folk are about; all idle wanderers, or so I suspect. No person of Garwiy is early for an event. Those who come to hear the scandal will arrive one minute before the chime."

"What if none arrive?" asked Etzwane in melancholy hopefulness.

"There will be some," said Ifness, "including the Faceless Man, who cannot be happily anticipating the occasion. He may even post a Discriminator to discourage the speech. I suspect, however, that he will listen, then act as circumstances dictate. We must stimulate him to push his 'explode' button."

"And when I retain my head?"

"The torc circuits must occasionally fail; he will conclude that such is the case and send forth other impulses. Remember the signal I have stipulated."

"Yes, yes," muttered Etzwane. "I hope he doesn't become dissatisfied with his explosive and shoot me with a gun."

"A risk we must take . . . The time is still twenty minutes to the chime. Let us stand in the shadows yonder and rehearse the matter of your address."

The midafternoon chime sounded. From the foliage came the "anonymous adventurer." Looking neither right nor left, walking with something of a swagger, he approached the rostrum. He went to the rear, climbed the white-glass steps, and approached the lectern. He stopped short to study the magenta-bordered notice on the green-glass surface.

It was the Faceless Man's reaction, and it read:

> Your advertisement has excited the interest of the ANOME himself. He requests discretion, that you may not jeopardize certain very sensitive investigations. The ANOME'S opinion is this: the Roguskhoi are a nuisance, a tribe of disreputable folk already on the decline. A person properly informed will stress the minor and transitory aspects of the matter, or he might even wish to discuss a subject of more general interest.

Etzwane put down the notice. He examined the faces that had collected around the rostrum. A hundred persons stood watching; as many more sat on benches. To the left stood Ifness; he had pulled a merchant's hood over his soft white hair and by some peculiar alteration of pose now seemed one with the others. Did the Faceless Man stand among the people present? Etzwane looked from face to face. There: that hollow-cheeked man with the lank black hair and burning eyes. Or that small man yonder with the high round forehead, the delicate mouth. Or the handsome Aesthete in the green cloak with the neat fringe of black beard along his jaw. Or the stern man in the plum-colored habit of the Eclectic Godhead. Others, still others.

Etzwane wasted a moment or two longer, steeling himself to immobility. The audience had now assembled. Etzwane leaned forward and began to speak, and because of the magenta-bordered notice he altered his remarks.

"In my advertisements I promised remarkable information; this I will provide—immediately." He held up the notice. "The illustrious Anome himself has demonstrated an interest in my remarks. Listen to his advice!" Etzwane read the notice in a studiously solemn voice; when he looked up, he saw that he had indeed interested his audience; they gazed at him in wonder. Ifness, so Etzwane saw, studied the crowd with care. He carried an inconspicuous camera and took many pictures.

Etzwane frowned at the document. "I am pleased that the Anome considers my ideas significant, especially since his other informants have misled him. 'A minor and transitory' nuisance? The Anome should take the head of the man who so deceived him. The Roguskhoi threaten everyone who now hears me. They are not 'a tribe of disreputable folk'—as the Anome innocently believes. They are ruthless, well-armed warriors, and they are sexual maniacs as well. Do you know their habit? They do not copulate normally; instead they seed a woman with a dozen imps which are born while she sleeps, and never again can she bear a human child—though she can bear another dozen imps. Every woman alive in Garwiy now may conceivably mother a brood or two of Roguskhoi imps.

"The Hwan Wildlands swarm with Roguskhoi. In the cantons bordering the Hwan it is an accepted fact that the Roguskhoi have been sent from Palasedra.

"The situation is remarkable, is it not? Reputable folk have implored the Anome to destroy these terrible creatures. He refuses; in fact, he takes their heads. Why? Ask yourself. Why does the Faceless Man, our protector, scoff at this peril?"

Vibrations jarred at the back of Etzwane's neck: the explosive circuit. The Faceless Man was angry. Etzwane swung around to maximize the vibrations. They ceased before he could make a fix as to their direction. He clenched his left hand: the signal to Ifness.

Ifness nodded and studied the crowd with even more intense interest than before.

Etzwane spoke on: "Why does the Faceless Man deprecate so imminent a threat? Why does he write a document urging me to 'discretion?' Friends, I ask a question; I do not answer it. Is the Faceless Man—"

The vibrations struck again. Etzwane swung around but again could not decide upon the source of the pulses. He looked straight at the cold-eyed man in green, who stared back at him, gravely intent.

The directional antenna, at least with respect to the killer pulses, was a failure. It was pointless to provoke the Faceless Man to a state where he might use a weapon less subtle. Etzwane modified the tone of his discourse. "The question I wish to ask is this: has the Faceless Man become old? Has he lost his zest? Should he perhaps pass on his responsibilities to a man with more energy and decision?"

Etzwane looked around the group to see who responded to the question. Here he was disappointed; the folk in the audience all looked around as well, more interested in the others than themselves. (They knew their own ideas; how did the others feel?)

Etzwane spoke on in a voice of spurious docility. He held up the magenta-bordered notice. "In deference to the Anome, I will reveal no more secrets. I may say that I am not alone in my concern; I speak for a group of persons dedicated to the safety of Shant. I go now to make my report. In a week I will speak again, when I hope to recruit others into this group."

Etzwane jumped down from the rostrum and to avoid idle questions set off at a brisk pace in the direction from which he had come. As he walked, he touched the switch in his torc to activate the echo circuit. From the shelter of the foliage he looked back. The Aesthete in green strolled after him without haste. Behind the Aesthete, no less casual, came Ifness. Etzwane turned, hurried on. A vibration struck against the right side of his neck: someone had sent out a questing radiation.

Etzwane went directly to the blue tile cottage north of Garwiy.

As he passed along Elemyra Way, east of the Corporation Plaza, his torc vibrated a second time, again as he entered the Avenue of the Thasarene Directors, again as he turned down the hedge-shaded lane. Once within the cottage Etzwane slipped out of the clumsy black cloak, unclasped the torc and set it on the table. Leaving the cottage by the back door, he went to where he could survey the road.

Half an hour passed. Along the lane came a man in a hooded dark green cloak. His eyes were very keen; he looked constantly right and left and occasionally down at an object he held in his hand. At the gap in the hedge he stopped short, the instrument in his hand resonating to the pulse echoed from Etzwane's torc inside the cottage.

Stealthy as a thief, the man looked up and down the lane, peered along the path at the cottage; slipping quickly through the gap, he took shelter behind a lime tree. Here stood Etzwane, who sprang forward. The man was enormously strong; Etzwane clung with feet and one arm and with the other slapped the man on the side of the neck with the needle-sack Ifness had supplied.

Almost at once the man's activity lessened; a moment later he fell to his hands and knees.

Ifness appeared; the two carried the limp body into the cottage. Ifness, instantly setting to work, removed the man's torc. Etzwane switched off the echo circuit of his own torc.

Ifness gave an exclamation of dissatisfaction and drew forth a tube of black explosive, which he regarded with vast displeasure.

The man had regained consciousness to find his arms and wrists bound. "You are not the Faceless Man, after all," said Ifness.

"I never claimed to be," said the captive in a cool voice.

"Who are you, then?"

"I am the Aesthete Garstang: a Director of the Corporation."

"It seems that you serve the Faceless Man."

"As do all of us."

"You more than the rest, to judge by your conduct, and by this control box." From the table Ifness picked up the instrument he had taken from Garstang's cloak: a metal box, three inches wide, an inch deep, four inches long. From the top of the case protruded a set of studs, each a different color. The ten squares of a read-out below displayed the colors of Etzwane's torc.

Below the read-out, on one hand, was a yellow

switch, the yellow of death. On the other was a red switch, the red of invisibility—in this case the red of the invisible person being sought.

Ifness set the box on the table. "How do you explain this?"

"It explains itself."

"The yellow button?" Ifness raised his eyebrows.

"Destroy."

"The red button?"

"Find."

"And your exact status?"

"I am what you already know me to be: a Benevolence of the Faceless Man."

"When are you expected to make your report?"

"In an hour or so." Garstang's answers came easily, in a voice without intonation.

"You report in person?"

Garstang gave a chilly laugh. "Hardly. I report into an electric voice-wire; I receive my instructions by postal delivery or through the same voice-wire."

"How many Benevolences are employed?"

"Another besides myself, so I have been told."

"The two Benevolences and the Faceless Man carry boxes such as this?"

"I don't know what the others carry."

Etzwane asked, "The Faceless Man and two Benevolences—only three persons—police all Shant?"

Garstang gave a disinterested shrug. "The Faceless Man could do the job alone, had he a mind."

For a moment there was silence. Ifness and Etzwane studied their captive, who returned the inspection with eyebrows raised in debonair unconcern. Etzwane asked, "Why won't the Faceless Man move against the Roguskhoi?"

"I have no more knowledge than you."

Etzwane said in a brittle voice, "For a man so near to death, you are very easy."

Garstang seemed surprised. "I see no cause to fear death."

"You tried to take my life. Why should I not take yours?"

Garstang gave him a stare of disdainful puzzlement. "I did not try to take your life. I had no such orders."

Ifness held up his hand urgently to still Etzwane's angry retort. "What in fact were your orders?"

"I was to attend the meeting in Pandamon Park; I was to note the speaker's code and follow him to his place of residence; I was there to gather information."

"But you were not instructed to take the speaker's head?"

Garstang started to reply, then turned shrewd, quick glances first toward Etzwane, then Ifness. A change seemed to come over his face. "Why do you ask?"

"Someone attempted to take my head," said Etzwane. "If it wasn't you, it was the Faceless Man."

Garstang shrugged, calculated. "That may well be. But it has nothing to do with me."

"Perhaps not," said Ifness politely. "But now there is no more time for conversation. We must prepare to meet whomever comes to find you. Please turn your back."

Garstang slowly rose to his feet. "What do you plan to do?"

"I will anesthetize you. In a short time, if all

goes well, you will be released."

In response Garstang flung himself sideways. He raised his leg in a grotesque prancing gait. "Look out!" screamed Etzwane. "He wears a leg-gun!"

Fire! Glare! Explosion through the cuffs of Garstang's elegant trousers: the tinkle of broken glass; then the thud of Garstang's dead body falling to the floor. Ifness, who had crouched, snatched and fired his hand-gun, stood looking down at the corpse. Etzwane had never seen him so agitated. "I have soiled myself," hissed Ifness. "I have killed what I swore to preserve."

Etzwane gave a snort of disgust. "Here you sob over this dead murderer; but on other occasions, when you might have saved someone, you looked aside."

Ifness turned him a yellow-eyed glare, then, after a moment, spoke in a calm and even voice. "The deed is done. What impelled him to act so desperately? He was helpless." For a moment he stood musing. "Many mysteries remain," he muttered. "Much is obscure." He made a peremptory gesture. "Search the body, drag it to the back shed. I must modify his torc."

An hour later Ifness stood back. "In addition to the 'explode' and 'echo' circuits, I discover a simple vibrator signal as well. I have installed an alarm to inform us when someone seeks Garstang. This time should not be far distant." He went to the door. The suns had rolled behind the Ushkadel; the soft dusk of Garwiy, suffused with a million colored glooms, settled over the land. "Before us now is a problem in tactics," said Ifness. "First, what have we acheived? A great deal, it seems to me. Garstang has convincingly denied all attempts to take your head, hence we may reasonably put the onus for these acts upon the Faceless Man. We may affirm, therefore, that he came to Pandamon Park and into the range of my camera. If we chose, we might attempt to identify and investigate each of the two hundred persons present—a tedious prospect, however.

"Secondly: What can we next expect of the Faceless Man? He awaits Garstang's report. In view of his failure to take the 'anonymous adventurer's' head, he will be curious, to say the least. Lacking news, he will become first annoyed, then concerned. I would guess that Garstang's report was due an hour ago; we can expect a signal to Garstang's torc in the near future. Garstang, of course, will not respond. The Faceless Man must then either send forth another Benevolence or go himself to find Garstang, using the locator-pulses.

"We have, in fact, a situation analogous to that of this morning. Instead of the 'anonymous adventurer' and his threatened sedition, we now have Garstang's torc to stimulate our quail into motion."

Etzwane gave a grudging acquiescence. "I suppose that this is reasonable enough."

Garstang's torc emitted a thin, clear sound, eerily disturbing the silence, followed by four staccato chirping noises.

Ifness gave a fateful nod. "There: the signal for Garstang to report at once. Time we were moving. The cottage gives us no advantage." He dropped Garstang's torc into a soft black case, then after reflecting a moment added a handful of his exquisite tools.

"If we don't hurry, we'll have the Discriminators around our ears," grumbled Etzwane.

"Yes, we must hurry. Switch off the echo circuit in your torc if you have not already done so."

"I have done so, long since."

The two departed the cottage and walked toward Garwiy's complicated skyline. Beyond, along the Ushkadel, a thousand palaces glittered and sparkled. Trudging through the dark with Ifness, Etzwane felt like a ghost walking with another ghost; they were two creatures on an eerie errand, estranged from all other folk of Shant. "Where are we going?"

Ifness said mildly, "To a public house, a tavern, something of the sort. We will put Garstang's torc in a secluded spot and watch to see who goes to investigate."

Etzwane could find no fault with the idea. "Fontenay's is yonder, along the river. Frolitz and the troupe will be there."

"As good as any. You, at least, will be provided the camouflage of your instrument."

Chapter 11

Music came through the open door of Fontenay's. Etzwane recognized the fluid lower register of Frolitz's wood-horn, the graceful touch of Fordyce's khitan, Mielke's grave bass tones; he felt a deprivation so great that tears came to his eyes. His previous life, so miserly and pinched, with every florin into his lock-box, now seemed sweet indeed!

They entered and stood in the shadows. Ifness surveyed the premises. "What is that door?"

"It leads to Fontenay's private quarters."

"What about the hall yonder?"

"It leads to the stairs and a back door."

"And what about that door behind Frolitz?"

"It leads into a storeroom where the musicians leave their instruments."

"It should serve. Take Garstang's torc, go into the storeroom for your instrument, and hang the torc somewhere near the door. Then when you come forth——" From within the black bag Garstang's torc produced the whine of the locator circuit. "Someone soon will be here. When you come forth, take a place near the storeroom door. I will sit in this corner. If you notice anything significant, look toward me, then turn your left ear toward what you notice. Do this several times, in case I do not see you the first time, as I will be busy otherwise. . . . Again, where is the rear entrance?"

"Down the hall, past the stairs and to the right."

Ifness nodded. "You are now a musician, a part of the troupe. Don't forget the torc."

Etzwane took the torc, tucked it into his inside pocket. He sauntered up to Frolitz, who gave him an indifferent nod. Etzwane recalled that he had been parted from the troupe only a single day. It seemed as if a month had passed. He went into the storeroom, hung the torc on a peg near the door, and covered it with someone's old jacket. He found his khitan, his tringolet, and his beautiful silver-mounted wood-horn and brought them out to the musician's platform. Finding a chair, he seated himself only a yard from the door. Ifness still sat in the corner of the room; with his mild expression he might have been a merchant's clerk; no one would look at him twice. Etzwane, playing with the troupe, was merged even more completely into the environment. Etzwane smiled sourly. The stalking of the Faceless Man was not without its ludicrous aspects.

With Etzwane present, Fordyce put aside his khitan and took up the bass clarion; Frolitz jerked his head in satisfaction.

Etzwane played with only a quarter of his mind. His faculties seemed magnified, hypersensitized. Every sound in the room reached his ears: every tone and quaver of music, the tinkle of glasses, the thud of mugs, the laughter and conversation. And from the storeroom an almost petulant whine from Garstang's torc. Etzwane glanced toward the far corner of the room; catching Ifness's eye, he reached up his hand as if to tune the khitan and gave a jerk of his thumb back toward the storeroom. Ifness nodded in comprehension.

The music halted. Frolitz turned around. "We will play that old piece of Anatoly's; you, Etzwane—" Frolitz explained a variation on the harmony. The barmen brought up mugs of beer; the musicians refreshed themselves. Etzwane thought: here was a life worth living—easy, relaxed, not a worry in the world. Except for the Roguskhoi and the Faceless Man. He lifted his mug and drank. Frolitz gave a sign; the music started. Etzwane let his fingers move of themselves; his attention wandered around the room. Fontenay tonight did good business; all the tables were occupied. The mulberry glass bosses high in the dark blue glass wall admitted a glow from the lights outside; over the bar hung a pair of soft white glow-bulbs. Etzwane looked everywhere, studying everyone: the folk coming through the door, Aljamo with fingers tapping the marimba-boards, the pretty girl who had come to sit at a nearby table, Frolitz now stroking a tipple, Ifness. Who among these people would know him now for the "anonymous adventurer" who had so disturbed the Faceless Man?

Etzwane thought of his past life. He had known much melancholy; his only pleasure had come from music. His gaze wandered to the pretty girl he had noticed before: an Aesthete, from the Ushkadel, or so he assumed. She wore clothes of elegant simplicity: a gown of dark scarlet-rose, a fillet of silver with a pair of rock crystals dangling past her ear, a curious jeweled belt, slippers of rose satin and pink glass. She was dark-haired, with a clever, grave face; never had Etzwane seen anyone so captivating. She felt his gaze and looked at him. Etzwane looked away, but now he played to her with new concentration and intensity. Never had he played so richly, with such lilting phrases, such poignant chords. Frolitz gave him a half-sneering side-glance, as if wordlessly asking, "What's got into you?" The girl leaned to whisper to her escort, whom Etzwane had hardly noticed: a man of early middle-age, apparently also an Aesthete. Behind Etzwane the torc gave a thin whine, reminding him of his responsibilities.

The Aesthete girl and her escort moved to a table directly in front of Etzwane, the escort glum-faced and bored.

The music halted. The girl spoke to Etzwane. "You play very well."

"Yes," said Etzwane with a modest smile. "I suppose I do." He looked toward Ifness, to find him frowning disapproval. Ifness had wished that particular table close by the storeroom left vacant. Etzwane again made the quick signal with his thumb toward the torc. Ifness nodded distantly.

Frolitz spoke over his shoulder: "The Merrydown." He jerked his head to give a beat; the music came forth, a rollicking quick-step, up and down, with unexpected halts and double beats. Etzwane's part was mainly a strong and urgent chord progression; he was able to watch the girl. She improved upon proximity. She gave off a subtle fragrance; her skin had a clean glow; she knew the uses of beauty as Etzwane knew the meaning of music. He thought with a sudden inner ferocity, "I want her; I must have her for my own." He looked at her, and his intent showed clear in his eyes. She raised her eyebrows and turned to speak to her escort.

The music ended; the girl paid no more heed

to Etzwane. She seemed uneasy. She settled her fillet, adjusted her belt. Behind Etzwane came the whine of the circuit. The girl jerked to stare. "What is that?" she asked Etzwane.

Etzwane pretended to listen. "I hear nothing."

"Is someone in there making peculiar sounds?"

"Perhaps a musician rehearsing."

"You are joking." Her face was alive with— humor? Alert mischief? Etzwane wondered.

"Someone is ill," she suggested. "You had better investigate."

"If you'll come in with me."

"No, thank you." She turned to her escort, who gave Etzwane a glance of haughty warning. Etzwane looked toward Ifness and, meeting his gaze, turned to look fixedly toward Frolitz, who stood to his right. His left ear indicated the table in front of him.

Ifness nodded without overmuch interest, or so it seemed to Etzwane.

Into the tavern came four men wearing mauve and gray uniforms: Discriminators. One spoke loudly: "Your attention! A disturbance has been reported in this building. In the name of the Corporation, I order no one to move."

Etzwane glimpsed the twitch of Ifness's hand. Two reports, two flashes: The glow-bulbs burst. Darkness and confusion came suddenly to Fontenay's tavern. Etzwane made a lunge. He felt the girl, caught her up, carried her in front of Frolitz into the hall. She tried to scream. Etzwane clapped his hand over her mouth. "Not a sound if you know what's good for you!" She kicked and struck at him; her noises were drowned by hoarse shouts in the tavern proper.

Etzwane staggered to the back door; he groped for the latch, opened the door, carried the writhing girl out into the night. Here he paused, let her feet swing to the ground. She tried to kick him. Etzwane twisted her around, held her arms in a lock. "No noise," he growled in her ear.

"What are you doing to me?" she cried.

"Keeping you safe from the raid. Such affairs are great inconveniences."

"You are the musician!"

"Exactly."

"Let me go back. I don't fear the Discriminators."

"What idiocy!" Etzwane exclaimed. "Now that we are free of that tiresome man you sat with, we can go elsewhere."

"No, no, no!" Her voice was more confident, even somewhat amused. "You are gallant and bold—but I must go back into the tavern."

"You may not," said Etzwane. "Come with me, and please make no trouble."

The girl once more became alarmed. "Where are you taking me?"

"You'll see."

"No, no! I—" Someone came behind; Etzwane turned, ready to drop the girl and defend himself. Ifness spoke, "Are you there?"

"Yes. With a captive."

Ifness approached. In the dim light of the back alley he peered at the girl. "Who do you have?"

"I can't say for sure. She wears a peculiar belt. I suggest you take it."

"No!" cried the girl in an astounded voice.

Ifness unclasped the belt. "We had best be away, and swiftly." He told the girl: "Do not make a scene of any sort; do not scream or try to attract attention or we will use you roughly. Is that understood?"

"Yes," she said huskily.

Each taking one of the girl's arms, they set off through the back streets and in due course arrived at the blue tile cottage. Ifness unlocked the door; they entered.

Ifness pointed to a couch. "Please sit."

The girl wordlessly obeyed. Ifness examined the belt. "Curious indeed."

"So I thought. I noticed her touch the red stud whenever the alarm sounded."

"You are observant," said Ifness. "I thought you were interested otherwise. Be careful of her; remember Garstang's leg-gun."

Etzwane went to stand by the girl. "No Faceless Man, then—but a Faceless Woman."

The girl made a scornful sound. "You are mad."

Ifness said gently, "Please turn and lay face down on the couch. Excuse me while I search for a weapon." He did so with thoroughness. The girl cried out in indignation; Etzwane looked away. "No weapons," said Ifness.

"You need only to have asked," said the girl. "I would have told you."

"You are not otherwise candid."

"You have asked no questions."

"I shall, in a few minutes." He rolled over his work table, adjusted the vise to grip the girl's torc. "Do not move or I will be forced to anesthetize you." He worked with his tools, opened her torc. Reaching with his long-nose pliers he removed a tube of explosive. "No Faceless Man, nor Faceless Woman, either," he told Etzwane. "You seized the wrong individual."

"This is what I tried to tell you," cried the girl in a voice of desperate hope. "It's all a terrible mistake. I am of the Xhiallinen; and I want nothing to do with you or your intrigues."

Ifness, making no response, worked further on the torc. "The echo circuit is dead. You cannot now be located. We can relax and test your vaunted candor. You are of the Xhiallinen family?"

"I am Jurjin of Xhiallinen." The girl spoke sullenly.

"And why do you wear this belt?"

"For the most simple reason imaginable: vanity."

Ifness went to the cupboard and returned with a small sac, which he pressed to the girl's neck: sides, nape, and front. She looked at him in apprehension. "It is wet. What did you do to me?"

"The liquid penetrates your skin and enters your blood. In a moment it will reach your brain and paralyze a certain small organ. Then we will talk further."

Jurjin's face became rueful and anxious. Etzwane watched her in morbid fascination, wondering as to the details of her existence. She wore her gown with flair and ease; she used the manners of the Garwiy patricians; her coloring was that of the Garwiy race. But her features showed a trace of some foreign strain. Xhiallinen, one of the Fourteen Families, was ancient, and if anything inbred. Jurjin spoke. "I will tell you the truth voluntarily, while I still can think. I wear the belt because the Anome required service of me, and I could not refuse."

"What was the service?"

"To act as Benevolence."

"Who are the other Benevolences?"

"There is only Garstang of Allingenen."

"Might there not be others?"

"I am certain that there are none."

"You, Garstang, and the Faceless Man controlled the whole of Shant?"

"The cantons and the cities are ruled by their particular leaders. It is only necessary to work through these folk. One alone could do this."

Etzwane started to speak, then controlled his voice. These slim hands must often have pressed the yellow stud of her belt; she must often have seen the heads of men disappear. He turned away with a heavy feeling in his throat.

"Who," asked Ifness ingenuously, "is the Faceless Man?"

"I don't know. He is as faceless to me as he is to you."

Ifness asked, "The box Garstang carried, and your belt: are they guarded against unauthorized use?"

"Yes. Gray must be pressed before the colors are coded."

Ifness leaned forward, inspected her eyes, and gave a slight nod. "Why did you summon the Discriminators to Fontenay's?"

"I did not summon them."

"Who did?"

"The Faceless Man, I suppose."

"Who was your escort?"

"The Second of Curnainen, Matheleno."

"Is he the Faceless Man?"

Jurjin's face showed a flicker of astonishment. "Matheleno? How could he be so?"

"Have you received orders from the Faceless

Man in regard to Matheleno?"

"No."

"He is your lover?"

"The Faceless Man said I might take no lovers."
Jurjin's voice began to slur; her eyelids drooped.

"Was the Faceless Man at Fontenay's Tavern?"

"I am not sure. I think he was there and noticed
something which impelled him to call in the Discriminators."

"What could that have been?"

"Spies."

"Spies from where?"

"From Palesedra." Jurjins voice came slowly;
her eyes took on a curious blank stare.

Ifness spoke sharply: "Why should he fear
Palasedrans?"

Jurjin's voice was an unintelligible mutter; her
eyes closed.

She slept. Ifness stood looking down in annoy-
ance.

Etzwane looked from Ifness to the girl and
back to Ifness. "What troubles you?"

"Her lapse into coma came swiftly. Too swiftly."

Etzwane peered into the girl's calm face. "She
could not feign such a thing."

"No." Ifness bent over Jurjin's face. He scrutinized each of her features, opened her mouth,
peered within. "Hmm."

"What do you see?"

"Nothing conclusive, or even suggestive."

Etzwane turned away, his mind inhabited only
by doubts and uncertainties. He straightened the
girl's body on the couch and drew a shawl over
her. Ifness watched with brooding detachment.

"What do we do now?" Etzwane asked. He no
longer felt antagonism toward Ifness; such an

emotion seemed pointless.

Ifness stirred, as if rousing from a reverie. "We return to a consideration of the Faceless Man and his identity—though for a fact other mysteries seem more cogent."

"Other mysteries?" Etzwane asked, uncomfortably aware that he must seem numb and stupid.

"There are several. First I might cite the Roguskhoi scimitars. Then Garstang for no clear or good reason attempts a desperate attack. Jurjin of Xhiallinen lapses into a coma as if her brain has been turned off. And the Faceless Man resists, not passively but actively, all demonstrations against the Roguskhoi. All seem guided by a transcendent policy beyond our present imagination."

"It is very strange," muttered Etzwane.

"Were the Roguskhoi human, we might reconcile these grotesque acts with simple treachery; but the concept of Garstang and Jurjin of Xhiallinen plotting with the Roguskhoi is sheer insanity."

"Not if the Roguskhoi are Palasedran freaks sent here to destroy us."

"The theory is arguable," said Ifness, "until someone troubles to examine the physiology of the Roguskhoi and considers their reproductive methods. Then doubt is renewed. However—to the lesser mystery. Who is the Faceless Man? We have thrown two stones; the quail has made two startled motions. To recapitulate: We are told with authority that the Anome employed only two Benevolences. Jurjin was not at Pandamon Park, yet an attempt was made to take your head. We must credit this attempt to the

Faceless Man. Garstang was not at Fontenay's, still someone summoned the Discriminators. Again we must hold the Faceless Man responsible. I took photographs at both locations; if we find a person common to both—well, let's see what the Laws of Probability have to tell us. I believe that I can quote precise odds. There are roughly two hundred thousand adults in this immediate area, of which two hundred heard the 'anonymous adventurer'—not a large turnout: one in each thousand persons. A similar number might have come to Fontenay's to enjoy the music of Frolitz's troupe: only about a hundred, or one in each two thousand did so. The chances of the same person being present at both locations—unless he had urgent business at both, as did you, I, and the Faceless Man—are therefore one in two million: sufficiently scant to discount. So then, let us investigate."

Ifness brought from his pocket a tube of dull black metal an inch in diameter, four inches long. Along the flattened top a number of knobs caught the light and glittered in Ifness's hand. He made an adjustment, pointed the tube at the wall beside Etzwane, and projected a cone of light.

Etzwane had never seen a photograph so detailed. He glimpsed several views of the Corporation Plaza; then Ifness made new adjustments, sending a thousand images flickering aginst the wall. The picture became still, to depict Pandamon Park and the folk who had come to hear the "anonymous adventurer."

"Look carefully at these faces," said Ifness. "Unfortunately I can't show these pictures and those from Fontenay's in juxtaposition; we must shift from one set to another."

Etzwane pointed: "There stands Garstang. Here—here—here—here—" he pointed to other faces. "I noticed these men; I wondered which might be the Anome."

"Study them. He will certainly know tricks of altering his appearance." Ifness projected pictures from various angles and vantages; together they scrutinized every face visible.

"Now to Fontenay's taproom."

The taproom was half-empty; the musicians sat on the dais. Matheleno and Jurjin had not yet occupied the table near Etzwane.

Ifness chuckled. "You chose a perfect disguise. You appear as yourself."

Etzwane, uncertain as to the quality of Ifness's amusement, gave a noncommittal grunt.

"We go forward in time. The young woman and Matheleno are at your table. Could Matheleno be one of the men at Pandamon Park?"

"No," said Etzwane after reflection. "He somewhat resembles Garstang, however."

"The Aesthetes are a distinctive group—a race, in fact, in the process of differentiating."

The picture changed once more. "It is now four to five minutes before the Discriminators arrived. I would suppose the Faceless Man to be in the room. He would stand where he could watch his Benevolence." Ifness expanded the cone of light, magnifying the images, sending some to the ceiling, some to the floor. Moving the projector, he brought the faces one at a time to the wall beside Etzwane.

Etzwane pointed. "The man in the far corner leaning against the bar."

Ifness expanded the image. They looked at the

face. It was a quiet face, broad of forehead, clever
of eye, small of chin and mouth. The man himself was short, trim, compact. His age could not
be guessed.

Ifness flicked back to Pandamon Park. Etzwane
pointed out the small man with the pursed mouth
and the clever sidelong eyes. "There he is."

"Yes," said Ifness. "That is he, unless my logic
and the laws of mathematics are at fault, and one
is as incontrovertible as the other."

For a period they studied the face of the Faceless Man.

"Now what?" Etzwane asked.

"For now—nothing. Go to bed, sleep. Tomorrow we will try to put a name to the fellow."

"What of her?" Etzwane indicated the dazed
girl.

"She won't move for twelve to fourteen hours."

Chapter 12

The suns tumbled up into the mauve autumn sky like rollicking kittens: Sasetta over Ezeletta behind Zael. Ifness left the cottage slowly and cautiously, like an old gray fox going forth to hunt. Etzwane sat elbows on knees, pondering Jurjin of Xhiallinen. She lay as Ifness had left her, breathing shallowly: a creature, Etzwane thought, of absolutely entrancing appearance, beautiful enough to hypnotize a man. He studied her face: the pure pale skin, the innocent profile, the dusky eyelashes. How to reconcile this Jurjin of Xhiallinen with her dark occupation? No question but what the work must be done by someone. If unlawful acts went unpunished, Shant would lapse into anarchy, as in the old days when canton feuded with canton. Etzwane's mind was a confusion, swinging between noble rationalization and disgust. She had been commanded by the Anome; she had no choice but to obey. But why had the Anome commanded her, Jurjin of Xhiallinen, to serve as his Benevolence? Surely men like Garstang were more apt for such a service. The Anome's mind was a labyrinth with many strange chambers. Like the minds of all men, including his own, Etzwane told himself bitterly.

He reached forth, arranged a lock of her soft dark hair. Her eyelids flickered and slowly opened. She turned her head and looked at Etzwane. "You are the musician."

"Yes."

She lay quiet, thinking. She noticed the light pouring through the window and made a sudden movement. "It is daytime; I can't stay here."

"You must."

"But why?" She turned him a melting glance. "I have done you no harm."

"You would, had you the chance."

Jurjin inspected Etzwane's dour face. "Are you a criminal?"

"I am the 'anonymous adventurer' that Garstang went forth to kill."

"You taught sedition!"

"I urged that the Faceless Man protect Shant from the Roguskhoi. That is not sedition."

"The Roguskhoi are nothing to be feared. The Anome has told us this."

Etzwane gave an angry ejaculation. "I saw the results of the raid on Bashon. My mother was killed."

Jurjin's face became blank and distant. She murmured, "The Roguskhoi are nothing to fear."

"How would you cope with them, then?"

Jurjin focused her eyes upon him. "I don't know."

"And when they swarm down upon Garwiy, what will you do then? Do you wish to be ravaged? Would you bear a dozen imps that creep from your body while you sleep?"

Jurjin's face twitched. She started to wail, stopped short and became placid. "It's a matter for the Anome." She raised to her elbow and, watching Etzwane, slowly slid her legs to the floor. Etzwane watched impassively. He asked, "Are you hungry, or thirsty?"

She made no direct reply. "How long will you keep me here?"

"Until we find the Faceless Man."

"What do you want with him?"

"We will insist that he deal with the Roguskhoi."

"You intend him no harm?"

"Not I," said Etzwane, "though he has unjustly tried to kill me."

"The acts of the Anome must always be just. What if you can't find him?"

"Then you will remain here. Could it be otherwise?"

"Not from your point of view. Why do you look at me like that?"

"I wonder about you. How many men have you killed?"

She screamed, "One less than I would wish to!" and sprang for the door. Etzwane sat watching. Ten feet from the couch she was jerked to a halt by the cord Ifness had tied from her waist to the couch. She cried out in pain, turned and tugged frantically at the cord. Etzwane watched with detachment, feeling no pity.

Jurjin found the knot too cunning for her fingers. Slowly she returned to the couch. Etzwane had no more to say to her.

So they sat for two hours. Ifness returned as quietly as he had gone. He carried a folder that he handed to Etzwane; it contained six large photographic prints, so detailed that Etzwane could count the hairs of the man's sparse eyelashes. At Pandamon Park he had worn a soft black rimless cap pulled low over his forehead; this, with his down-curving little mouth and small, almost im-

mature, nose, gave his face a foreshortened bull-
dog look. At Fontenay's the dark hair of a wig
was drawn straight back from his forehead to
swirl down and around each ear: a style popular
among the upper middle classes of Garwiy, which
displayed to advantage the philosopher's forehead and diminished the pinched expression of
nose and mouth. Nowhere did the eyes look directly ahead; always they bore off somewhat to
right or left. In both sets of photographs he appeared humorless, determined, introspective, and
pitiless.

Etzwane studied the pictures until the face was
stamped into his consciousness. He returned the
pictures to Ifness.

Jurjin, sitting on the couch, feigned boredom.
Ifness handed her the photographs. "Who is this
man?"

Jurjin's eyelids descended the merest twitch;
she said in a voice rather too casual, "I haven't a
notion."

"Have you ever seen him?"

Jurjin frowned and licked her lips. "I see many
people; I couldn't begin to remember them all."

Ifness asked, "If you knew this man's identity,
would you tell us?"

Jurjin laughed. "Of course not."

Ifness nodded and went to the wall cabinet.
Jurjin watched him, her mouth sagging in dismay. Ifness asked over his shoulder, "Are you
hungry or thirsty?"

"No."

"Do you care to visit the bathroom?"

"No."

"You had best consider carefully," said Ifness.

"It now becomes necessary that I apply the hypnotic tincture. You will not move for twelve hours, which, added to the twelve hours you have already occupied the couch, might cause an embarrassment."

"Very well," said Jurjin in a cold voice. "Be so good as to release me; I would like to wash my face and hands."

"Of course." Ifness untied the cord; Jurjin marched to the door Ifness indicated. Ifness spoke to Etzwane, "Stand below the bathroom window."

A moment after Etzwane arrived at his post the window eased cautiously ajar, and Jurjin looked out. At the sight of Etzwane she scowled and closed the window once more.

Jurjin returned slowly to the living room. "I do not care to be drugged," she told Ifness in a flippant voice. "Dreadful dreams afflict me."

"Indeed! What do you dream about?"

"I don't remember. Frightening things. I become very sick."

Ifness was unmoved. "I will dose you more heavily."

"No, no! You want to ask me about the pictures! I'll help you any way I know!" Her bravado had disappeared; her face had melted; it was tender, beseeching. Etzwane wondered how she looked with her finger on the yellow button.

Ifness asked, "Are you concealing information regarding the pictures?"

"Suppose I were? Would you expect disloyalty of me?"

"No," said Ifness. "I use the drug and remove your options. Please return to the couch."

"You will make me sick. I will fight you; I will kick and scream and bite."

"Not for long," said Ifness.

The sobbing girl lay on the couch. Etzwane, panting, sat on her knees and pressed down on her arms. Ifness applied the solution to her neck. Almost at once her writhing halted.

Ifness asked, "What do you know of the man in the photograph?"

Jurjin lay in a coma.

Etzwane said in a hushed voice, "You dosed her too heavily."

"No," said Ifness. "An overdose has no such effect."

"Then what happened to her?"

"I am mystified. First Garstang chooses an absurd method of suicide, now this."

"Do you think she knows the Faceless Man?"

"No. But she knows the man in the photographs. The Aesthetes, after all, are not strangers to each other." Ifness studied the photographs. "Of course, he might be the green-grocer. I neglected to mention that a picture of the 'anonymous adventurer' is posted in the Corporation Plaza, with information requested by the Discriminators."

"Hmf. So now I am proscribed."

"Until we remonstrate with the Faceless Man."

"He will be on his guard, with both Benevolences missing."

"So I would imagine. The identity of his adversaries must puzzle him greatly."

"Jurjin mentioned Palasedran spies."

"Similar theories may occur to the Faceless Man." Ifness studied the photographs. "Notice his torc. Observe the colors. What do they signify?"

"The purple-green is Garwiy. Double dark green is a person without trade or craft: a landholder, an industrialist, a foreign trader, an Aesthete."

Ifness nodded placidly. "No new information. The torc will certainly not respond to an echo pulse. No doubt we could walk about the Ushkadel asking questions, but I fear that we would soon be approached by the Discriminators."

Etzwane studied the photographs. "He travels around Shant, at least to some extent. Balloon-way clerks might recognize his picture."

"But would they give us information? Or would they consult the Discriminators?"

"The publishers of *Frivolity* no doubt could put a name to him, but I suppose the same objection applies."

"Precisely. Questions arouse suspicion. Before informing a pair of strangers, they would first notify the principal."

Etzwane pointed to the collar of the Faceless Man's jacket. "Notice this brooch: silver and amethyst in a clever design. The artificers of such objects occupy Neroi Square, to the west of Corporation Plaza. The maker would be certain to recognize his work. When we put forth the story that we had found the jewel, he might supply the name of the person to whom he had sold it."

"Excellent," said Ifness. "We will try this plan."

Neroi Square occupied the heart of the Old City. The paving—three-foot tiles of murky lavender glass—was worn and irregular; the fountain at the center dated from the reign of the first Caspar Pandamon. A two-story arcade of translucent black glass surrounded the square, each column displaying the emblem of a mercantile family extinct two thousand years. The old offices had been converted into workshops for Garwiy's jewelers and metal-crafters. Each worked jealously alone, with his sons and nephews for apprentices, barely deigning to recognize the existence of his fellows. The work of each shop reflected the temperament of the shop-elder; some were known for their opals, agates, moonstones; others carved tourmaline or beryl; others created miniatures with microscopic slivers of cinnabar, lapis, turquoise, jade. Fashions and whimsicalities were only grudgingly heeded; special orders were accepted without enthusiasm. No piece carried seal or sigil; each craftsman deemed his work instantly recognizable.

The shop of Zafonce Agabil was currently in the mode; his designs were thought quaint and endearing. Into the shop of Zafonce Agabil went Ifness and Etzwane. Upon the counter Ifness tossed a section cut from his photograph of the Faceless Man. "Someone lost such a brooch at my house; did you make it? If so can you supply me the name of its owner, that I may return it?"

The clerk, one of the four Agabil sons, examined the photograph with a contemptuous twist of the mouth. "None of our work, certainly."

"Whose might it be?"

"I could not say."

At the shop of Lucinetto, Ifness encountered a similar response, but additionally: "It is somewhat old-fashioned work and might well be an heirloom. The cabochon is cut with an overly shallow dome, as one might use a garnet. Not our work; never, never, could we so shame a stone."

From shop to shop went Ifness and Etzwane.

At Meretrice's the latest of the lineage examined the photograph. "Yes, this is one of our pieces, in the style of the Siume Dynasty. Notice the vitality of the cabochon? It comes of a secret contour, known only to us. It was lost? A pity. I do not recall the purchaser; it was crafted five years or more ago."

"I think I know the owner," said Ifness. "He came as a friend of one of my guests, and I do not recall his name." He displayed a photograph of the Faceless Man.

Meretrice glanced at it. "Yes! That is Sajarano of Sershan Palace: something of a recluse. I am surprised he came to your banquet."

Chapter 13

The Sershan Palace, an intricate confection of clear and colored glass, faced southeast across Garwiy. Ifness and Etzwane examined the premises from a discreet distance. They saw no activity on the loggia nor in that area of the garden accessible to view. The Office of Archives had yielded information of no great interest. The Sershan lineage went back to middling antiquity. Prince Varo Sershan of Wild Rose had supported Viana Paizifume; a certain Almank Sershan had raided the south coast of Caraz, returning with a vast fortune in silver corpse effigies. Sajarano was last in the direct lineage. A spouse had died twenty years before without issue; he had never taken another. He still controlled the hereditary Wild Rose estates and was a keen agriculturist. Heir presumptive was a cousin, Cambarise of Sershan.

"One possible tactic is to go to the door and ask to speak to his Excellency Sajarano," said Ifness. "Such an approach, with the virtue of utter simplicity, has much to recommend it. A pity," he said in musing afterthought, "that my mind always discovers hazards and contingencies. What if he expects us? By no means impossible. Meretrice might have become suspicious. The clerk at the Office of Archives seemed overly alert."

"I believe he would call Discriminators the instant we appeared," said Etzwane. "Were I Sajarano I would be a worried man."

Ifness said, "In this same vein, were I Sajarano, I would not keep to my palace. I would dress inconspicuously and wander the city. We are wasting our time here. We should go where the Faceless Man is likely to go."

During the late afternoon the cafés of Corporation Plaza became crowded with folk making rendezvous; at the largest of these cafés Ifness and Etzwane seated themselves and ordered wine and biscuits.

The folk of Garwiy passed back and forth, all in greater or lesser degree imbued with the peculiar Garwiy verve and volatility.

They saw nothing of Sajarano.

The suns rolled behind the Ushkadel; shadows filled the plaza. "Time we were returning," said Ifness. "Jurjin will be rousing herself; we should be on hand."

Jurjin had already regained consciousness. Frantically, by every resource known to her, she had been trying to free herself from the cord that connected her waist to the couch. Her gown was disheveled where she had tried to slip the loop over her hips. The wood of the couch was scarred where she had sought to fray the cord. The knots, sealed by a means known only to Ifness, now engrossed her to such an extent that she failed to notice the arrival of Ifness and Etzwane. She looked up with the face of a trapped animal. "How long will you keep me here? I am miserable; what right have you to do such a thing to me?"

Ifness made a gesture of boredom. He loosened

the cord from the couch, allowed her once more the freedom of the house.

Etzwane prepared a meal of soup, bread, and dried meat, which at first she haughtily declined, then ate with good appetite.

She became more cheerful. "You two are the strangest men on Durdane. Look at you! Glum as crakes! Of course! You are ashamed of the acts you have perpetrated upon me!"

Ifness ignored her; Etzwane merely gave a sour chuckle.

"What are your plans?" she demanded. "Must I stay here forever?"

"Possibly," said Ifness. "I suspect however that circumstances may change in a day or two."

"And in the meantime? What of my friends? They are worried sick, of this I am sure. And must I wear this same gown day in and day out? You treat me like a beast."

"Patience," murmured Ifness. "Presently I will give you a drug and send you back to sleep."

"I do not want to sleep. I consider you the epitome of boorishness. And you—" she turned her attention upon Etzwane "—have you no gallantry? You sit grinning like a dogfish. Why do you not force the old man to release me?"

"So that you could report us to the Faceless Man?"

"It would be my duty. Should I be punished on this account?"

"You should not have become a Benevolence were you not willing to assume the risks."

"But I had no choice! One day I was told my destiny, and from that time my life was not my own."

"You could have refused to serve. Do you enjoy taking men's heads away from them?"

"Bah," she said, "you refuse to speak on a sensible level. What is wrong with you?" This to Ifness, who had jerked around in his chair, to sit listening.

Etzwane listened as well, but the night was quiet. "What do you hear?" he asked.

Ifness jumped to his feet. He went to the doorway and looked out into the dark. Etzwane rose as well. Still he could hear no sound. Ifness spoke in an incomprehensible language, then listened once more.

Jurjin took advantage of the distraction to coil the cord in her hand. She lunged for Ifness, hoping to push him aside and win her freedom. Etzwane, waiting for just such a move, caught her and carried her kicking and yelling to the couch. Ifness brought over his drug; the girl became quiet. Ifness tied the end of the rope to the couch, and this time taught Etzwane the secret of the lock. "The knot itself is a meaningless tangle of loops and turns." Ifness spoke in haste. "Come here to the table. I must teach you what I know of the torcs. Quickly now, quickly!"

"What is the trouble?"

Ifness looked toward the door. He spoke in a dreary voice: "I have been recalled. I am in deep disgrace. At the least I will be expelled from the Institute."

"How do you know all this?" demanded Etzwane.

"A signal has reached me. My time on Durdane is ended."

Etzwane stared with a slack jaw. "What of the Faceless Man? What shall I do?"

"Your best. It is tragic that I must go. Attend

me. I will leave you my tools, my weapons, my drugs. You must listen carefully, as I can explain only once. First: the torcs. Watch how to open one safely." He demonstrated on a torc he had brought from Gargamet Meadow. "And here is how to lock it. Watch; I will reactivate the girl's torc. The dexax fits in here; this is the detonator. The echo circuit is broken; notice this loose connection . . . Demonstrate what I have told you . . . Good . . . This is my only weapon; it shoots a needle of energy. The camera I must keep."

Etzwane listened with foreboding. He had not realized his dependence on the detestable Ifness. "Why must you leave?"

"Because I must! Be wary of the Faceless Man and his Benevolence here. Their conduct is aberrant, in an almost imperceptible degree."

A soft sound reached Etzwane's ears. Ifness heard it as well and turned his head; otherwise he made no move.

A polite rap-tap-tap sounded at the door. Ifness walked across the room, drew the latch. In the darkness stood two shapes. The first came a little forward; Etzwane saw a man of medium stature with a pale complexion, the blackest of hair and eyebrows. He seemed to smile, a placid, grim smile; his eyes glittered in the light. The second man was a vague shape in the gloom.

Ifness spoke in a language strange to Etzwane; the black-haired man replied curtly. Ifness spoke again; the stranger as before replied with a few dry syllables.

Ifness turned back into the cottage. He took his soft black case; without a glance, word, or gesture toward Etzwane, he stepped out into the night. The door closed.

A minute later Etzwane heard the soft sound. It faded into a sigh and was gone.

Etzwane poured himself a glass of wine and sat at the table. Jurjin of Xhiallinen lay in a coma on the couch.

Etzwane rose to his feet and explored the cottage. In the cabinet he found a wallet containing several thousand florins. In a wardrobe were garments: at need, they would fit Etzwane.

He went back to sit at the table. He thought of Frolitz, of the old days that in retrospect seemed so carefree. No more, never again. By now the "anonymous adventurer" must be identified with Gastel Etzwane.

He decided he did not wish to remain in the cottage. He slipped into Ifness's gray cape and a gray hat. Into his pocket he tucked the energy gun and Garstang's box. After a moment's deliberation he included the drug of stupefaction that Ifness had demonstrated to him: suppose he should meet Sajarano of Sershan on this autumn evening?

Etzwane turned down the lights. The cottage was dark except for the colored loom of Garwiy through the window. Jurjin lay quiet; he could not hear her breathing. Etzwane walked softly from the cottage.

For hours he wandered the avenues of Garwiy, pausing by cafés to examine the patrons, stepping into taverns to scan the faces in the room. He dared not approach Fontenay's. At midnight he ate a meat bun and a cake of cheese at a late-hour booth.

Mist had come drifting in from the Green Ocean. It flew in wafts and tendrils among the spires, blurring the colored lights, bringing a damp scent to the air. Few folk were abroad. Wrapping himself in the cloak, Etzwane returned to the cottage.

At the gate he halted. The dark cottage seemed to wait for him. Behind, in a shed, festered Garstang's body.

Etzwane listened. Silence, darkness. He walked through the garden and paused by the door. A slight sound? He strained his ears. Another sound: a dry scraping. Etzwane flung open the door, sidled into the room, gun in hand. He turned up the lights. No changes were evident. The back door creaked. Etzwane ran from the front door, circled the cottage. He saw nothing. The door of the shed appeared to be ajar. Etzwane stopped short, hair bristling at the nape of his neck. Slowly he approached; jumping forward, he slammed the door and threw the latch. Then he wheeled and sprang nervously aside in case the open door were a ploy to distract him.

No sound. Etzwane could not bring himself to investigate the shed. He went into the house. Jurjin lay in her coma. She had moved or been moved; an arm hung down to the floor.

Etzwane bolted the doors and drew the blinds. The cord binding Jurjin to the couch had been disturbed. The wooden frame of the couch had been abraded, rasped. Etzwane bent over Jurjin, examined her with care. He raised her eyelid. The eyeball was rolled back. Etzwane jerked around, looked over his shoulder.

The room was empty, save for the ghosts of dead conversations.

Etzwane brewed tea and went to sit in a chair. Time passed. Constellations rose and fell; Etzwane dozed. He awoke cold and stiff to find the light of dawn seeping through the shutters.

The cottage was quiet and dismal. Etzwane prepared himself a meal and planned his day. First he must examine the shed.

Jurjin awoke. She had nothing to say. He fed her and allowed her a visit to the bathroom. She returned in a dull and despondent mood, without defiance or vivacity. She stood in the center of the room flexing her arms, which apparently were cramped. Presently she asked, "Where is the old man?"

"He is gone about his affairs."

"What may they be?"

"You'll learn in due course."

"What a strange pair you are!"

"I find you much stranger than myself," said Etzwane. "By contrast I am starkly simple."

"But still you preach sedition."

"By no means. The Roguskhoi killed my mother, and my sister as well. I say that they must be destroyed, to save all of Shant. This is not sedition. It is ordinary rationality."

"You should leave such decisions to the Anome."

"He refuses to act; hence I must force him."

"The old man's mother was likewise killed?"

"I don't believe so."

"Why is he so zealous to break the laws?"

"From sheer philanthropy."

"What? That man? He is cold as the Nimmir wind."

"Yes, in certain ways he is strange. Now I must drug you once more."

Jurjin made an airy gesture. "You need not bother. I will agree not to leave the cottage."

Etzwane gave a cynical laugh. "Please be good

enough to lie upon the couch."

Jurjin approached him, smiling up into his face. "Let us be friends instead. Kiss me."

"Hmmf. At this time in the morning?"

"Would you like to?"

Etzwane dourly shook his head. "No."

"Am I so ill-favored? Old and wrinkled?"

"No. But if you could press the yellow button and take my head, you would do so. The idea does not compel my affection. Please make haste."

Jurjin thoughtfully went to the couch. She lay supine while Etzwane applied the drug, and soon she slept. Etzwane locked the cord to a decorative ceiling bracket.

He went out to inspect the shed. The door was bolted as before. He walked around. Nothing larger than a rat could have found its way in or out.

Etzwane flung wide the door; daylight revealed garden tools, household clutter, Garstang's body where he had dragged it. The face and chest were fearfully torn. Etzwane stood in the doorway looking for the creature that had done the damage. He did not dare enter for fear the rat, if such it were, might dart forth and bite him. He closed and bolted the door.

Wearing the gray cloak, Etzwane sauntered glumly into Garwiy. He went directly to the Corporation Plaza. The Faceless Man might be walking the halls of Sershan Palace. He might be resting in solitude at his Wild Rose estate. He might have gone off to the far corners of Shant to punish malefactors. Etzwane thought otherwise. If he were the Faceless Man, he would stay in Garwiy, in contact with the Discriminators, and sooner or later he must cross the Corporation Plaza.

Etzwane stood a moment or two under the old Clockmakers' Gate. A misty, chilly morning today, the suns eclipsing each other as they sidled across the sky. Etzwane went to a nearby café and took an inconspicuous table. He ordered broth and sat sipping.

The folk of Garwiy passed across the plaza. Near the Office of Petitions three Discriminators came together and stood talking. Etzwane watched them with interest. What if they all came at him together? He could never kill them all with the metal box; there would be insufficient time. The Faceless Man must carry another weapon, thought Etzwane; a device that would explode any torc at which it was pointed. Into the café came a man in a suit of gray and purple. His forehead was broad and pallid; the small nose, the pursed down-curving mouth were undistinguished, but the eyes, which looked off to the side, were luminous and thoughtful. He signaled to the waiter for a mug of soup; a motion peremptory but polite, in the fashion of the Aesthetes.

When the broth was served, he glanced sidewise toward Etzwane, who took care to have his own mug raised before his face; but for an unsettling instant he met the gaze of the Faceless Man.

The Faceless Man frowned slightly and looked away, as if resenting a stranger's attention.

Etzwane's nervousness made careful thinking difficult. He clenched the mug and, forcing his thoughts into a channel, sorted out his options.

He carried a gun. He could step forward, press it into the Anome's back, and utter appropriate orders. The plan had a single overwhelming disadvantage: conspicuity. If the act were noticed, as it must be, the Discriminators would be summoned.

He could wait until the Anome departed and follow; but the Anome in his present condition of uncertainty might well notice and lead him into a trap. Etzwane told himself that he must not relinquish the initiative.

The Anome, if he recognized the "anonymous adventurer," might be persuaded to follow Etzwane; more likely he would summon the Discriminators.

Etzwane heaved a fateful sigh. He reached into the pocket of his cape and secured an item of the equipment Ifness had left with him. He clinked a florin down on the table to pay for the broth; scraping his chair back, he rose to his feet; then, with an exclamation, he stumbled forward to place his hand upon the Faceless Man's neck. "Sir, my apologies!" declared Etzwane. "What a disgrace! This wet napkin has fallen upon your neck!"

"No matter, no matter."

"Allow me to help you."

The Anome jerked away. "You are clumsy; what do you mean daubing my neck in such a fashion?"

"Again, my apologies! I will replace your coat if it is stained."

"No, no, no. Just be off with you, I can take care of myself."

"Very well, sir, as you wish. I must explain

that this cursed chair engaged my leg and threw me forward. I'm sure the matter came as a great shock!"

"Yes, quite so. But the episode is finished; please say no more."

"Your indulgence one more moment; I must adjust my shoe. May I sit here no more than an instant?"

"As you will." The Anome turned away in his chair. Etzwane, dealing with his shoe, watched him carefully.

A moment passed. The Anome glanced about. "You are still here?"

"Yes. What is your name?"

The Anome blinked. "I am Sajarano of Sershan."

"Do you know me?"

"No."

"Look at me!"

Sajarano turned his head. His face was calm and even.

"Rise to your feet," said Etzwane. "Come with me."

Sajarano's face showed no emotion. Etzwane led him from the café.

"Walk faster," said Etzwane. They passed under the Pomegranate Portal into Serven Airo Way. Etzwane now clasped Sajarano's arm. Sajarano blinked. "I am tired."

"You will rest shortly. "Who is the 'anonymous adventurer?' "

"He is a man from the east; he is at the center of a seditious cabal."

"Who are the others of this cabal?"

"I don't know."

"Why do you not order soldiers against the Roguskhoi?"

Sajarano for ten seconds made no reply. Then he mumbled: "I don't know." His voice had begun to slur; he moved with an unsteady gait. Etzwane supported him and took him along the way as fast as possible, until near the Gate of the Seasons the Faceless Man could walk no more.

Etzwane conveyed him to a bench and waited until an empty fiacre came by, which he halted. "My friend has had a drop too much; we must take him home before his wife finds out."

"It happens to the best of us. Into the back with him. Can you manage?"

"Very well. Drive out the Avenue of the Thasarene Directors."

Chapter 14

Etzwane undressed the Faceless Man to his undergarments and laid him on the couch across from Jurjin. The Faceless Man was not physically impressive. From the garments Etzwane removed an activating box like that carried by Garstang, an energy gun of complex design, a small case that Etzwane presumed to be a radio transceiver, a metal tube of unknown function; Etzwane thought it might be the all-torc destroyer he had hypothesized.

He brought forth Ifness's tools and ranged them carefully in a row. With intense concentration he removed Sajarano's torc as he had seen Ifness do. To his intense puzzlement the torc contained a full complement of dexax. The echo circuits were apparently operative. Etzwane stared in amazement. What could be the reason for this? A terrible presentiment struck him; had he captured the wrong man?

If not, why should the Faceless Man wear an armed torc?

The solution rose into his mind—a reason so simple and full of relief that he laughed outright. Like everyone else Sajarano of Sershan had assumed his torc at puberty. When, through circumstances shrouded and secret, he had become the Anome, he knew no method to alter the situation, except to alter the color coding as protection against his Benevolences.

Etzwane slipped off his own torc. He restored the explosive to its slot, reconnected the circuits. He placed this around Sajarano's neck and locked it in place.

An unpleasant task awaited him. He went out to the shed and threw open the door. The rat, if such it were, scuttled under a pile of sacks. It had, so Etzwane noted, been feeding upon Garstang's body. In revulsion Etzwane brought forth Ifness's gun and sent a spear of pale fire at the sacks. They disappeared in a gust of vile-smelling smoke, and with them the creature who had taken refuge below.

Etzwane picked up a spade and, digging a shallow grave, buried Garstang.

When he returned into the house, all was as before. He bathed, changed his clothes, then sat and waited, his mood a strange mixture of exultation and loneliness.

Jurjin awoke first. She seemed tired; her face sagged and her skin showed an unhealthy color. Sitting up on the couch, she looked at Etzwane with undisguised bitterness.

"How long will you keep me here?"

"Not long now."

She peered across the room "Who is that man?"

"Do you know him?"

Jurjin shrugged, a brave attempt at debonair defiance.

"His name is Sajarano of Sershan," said Etzwane. "He is the Faceless Man."

"Why is he here?"

"You shall see. . . . Are you hungry?"

"No."

Etzwane thought a moment or two. Then he unlocked the cord that bound her. She stood up, free of her bonds. Etzwane faced her.

"Do not leave this house. If you do, I will take your head. The Anome is here and cannot help you. You must now obey me as formerly you did the Anome. You must not obey him. Do you understand?"

"I understand well enough. But I am confused. Who are you?"

"I am Gastel Etzwane, a musician. So I was, so I hope to be again."

Hours passed. Jurjin wandered about the house, watching Etzwane with wonder, defiance, and female spite.

Toward evening Sajarano recovered his senses. He became alert very quickly and sat up on the couch. For half a minute he appraised Etzwane and Jurjin. He spoke in the coldest of voices. "Suppose you explain why you have brought me here."

"Because the Roguskhoi must be attacked; because you refused to act."

"This is solemn and deliberate policy," said Sajarano. "I am a man of peace; I refuse to bring the horrors of war to Shant."

"Worry no longer; the Roguskhoi have done the job for you."

Etzwane pointed to Sajarano's old torc. "You are wearing an active torc. It carries its full complement of dexax. I carry the detonator. You now must answer to me, and your Benevolence as well."

Jurjin, standing across the room, went to sit on the couch. "I obey the Anome."

Sajarano asked, "What of Garstang?"

"Garstang is dead."

Sajarano's hand went up to his new torc, after the manner of the folk of Shant. "What do you propose to do?"

"The Roguskhoi must be destroyed."

Sajarano spoke in a quiet voice: "You do not know what you are saying. In Shant we enjoy peace and good fortune; we must maintain it. Why risk chaos and militarism for the sake of a few barbarians?"

"Peace and good fortune are not the natural bounties of nature," said Etzwane. "If you believe this, I will send you to Caraz where you can learn for yourself."

"You cannot wish to bring turmoil to Shant," cried Sajarano in a suddenly brassy voice.

"I wish to repel a clear and present danger. Will you obey my orders? If you refuse, I will kill you this moment."

Sajarano sank back in his chair. He seemed apathetic and watched Etzwane sidelong, in which pose his small nose and mouth seemed curiously immature. "I will obey."

Jurjin was restless; her face twitched and jerked in grimaces that under other circumstances might have been amusing. She rose to her feet, went to the table.

Etzwane asked, "The Discriminators are now searching for the 'anonymous adventurer?'"

"Yes."

"They have orders to kill him?"

"If necessary."

Etzwane gave him the transceiver. "How do you use this?"

Jurjin came forward as if interested. From behind her back flashed a glass knife. Etzwane, watching from the corner of his eye, knocked her sprawling back on the couch. Sajarano struggled up, kicked Etzwane, grappled him around the neck. Etzwane lunged ahead. The line around Sajarano's neck snapped taut, and snatched him flailing back to the couch.

"Your promises seem to mean little," Etzwane observed in a mild voice. "I was hoping that I might trust you both."

"Why should we not fight for what we believe?" demanded Jurjin.

"I promised to obey you," said Sajarano. "I said nothing about not trying to kill you when opportunity offered."

Etzwane grinned, a dour, sardonic grin. "In that case I order you not to try to kill or injure me in any way. Will you obey?"

Sajarano sighed in vast unease. "Yes. What else can I say?"

Etzwane looked at Jurjin. "What about you?"

"I promise nothing," she declared haughtily.

Etzwane seized her arm and pulled her toward the door.

"Where are you going?" she cried. "What are you doing?"

"I am taking you to the back yard to kill you," said Etzwane.

"No, no no!" she cried. "Please do not. I promise to obey you!"

"And will you seek to harm me?"

"No!"

Etzwane released her; she ran back to the couch.

Etzwane returned to Sajarano. "Explain the function of this transceiver."

"I press the white button," said Sajarano in a calm voice. "It transmits to the relays I designate on this dial. I speak; the orders are broadcast from the relay station."

"Call the Discriminators, order them no longer to molest the 'anonymous adventurer.' State that Gastel Etzwane must be given respectful and instant obedience, no less than you would expect for yourself."

Sajarano did so in a flat voice. He looked up at Etzwane. "What else do you require of me?"

Etzwane, standing across the room, looked from one face to the other, from Jurjin of Xhiallinen to the Faceless Man. Both, he knew, would play him false as soon as opportunity offered. Dead, they would be no threat to him. Jurjin's eyes widened as if she read his thoughts. It might be for the best. Still, if he killed the Faceless Man, who would govern Shant? Who would organize the military apparatus necessary to his goals? The Faceless Man must live; in which case he could see no reason to kill Jurjin of Xhiallinen.

The two watched him intently, trying to divine the direction of his thoughts. Etzwane said in a fateful voice: "You are free to go. Do not leave the Ushkadel."

He untied the cord from Sajarano's waist. "A warning: if I am killed, my associates will still take both your heads."

With neither ceremony nor overmuch dignity the two departed the cottage. At the gate Jurjin looked over her shoulder; in the dark Etzwane could see only the glimmer of her face. Uneasily he sensed that Ifness would have handled the situation differently, that at some essential juncture his affairs had gone wrong.

He loaded Ifness's black case with such weapons and instruments he did not dare leave behind and departed the cottage.

At the Old Pagane he dined on the best the house offered, amused by his twinges of instinctive parsimony. Money had become the least of his concerns.

He sauntered along the river bank to Fontenay's where he found Frolitz and the troupe drinking beer. Frolitz hailed Etzwane in angry reproof mixed with relief. "What have you been up to? We've been persecuted by the Discriminators! They say you kidnaped an Aesthete girl."

"All nonsense," said Etzwane. "A ridiculous mistake. I'd rather not talk about it."

"Clearly you don't care to enlighten us," said Frolitz. "Well, no matter: to work. I have a sore lip; tonight I'll use the khitan; Etzwane will play wood-horn. We'll start with that Morningshore trifle 'Birds in the Surf.'"